A MARCHIONESS FOR CHRISTMAS

ALANNA LUCAS

ISBN 978-1-956367-00-3

Sebastiani Press

PO Box 1234

Simi Valley, Ca 93062

Cover by Dar Albert

For my mom, with love.
Thank you for introducing the violin to me ♪♫♪

CHAPTER 1

*A*ntonia stared down at the nearly finished needlework resting in her lap. The white fabric and intricate mistletoe design with its white pearl seeds was a stark contrast to her widow's weeds. Sadness she had managed to keep at bay throughout the year always crept up at the beginning of Advent. Singing carols, decorating the house on Christmas Eve with keepsakes, and bringing in the Yule log had all been cherished traditions. Indeed, Christmastide had been her favorite season until six years ago when her mother passed away days before Christmas Eve. The loss was compounded by her father's lack of compassion. Closing her eyes, Antonia tried to block the images of her mother on her deathbed.

"Mrs. Tomlin. I say, Mrs. Tomlin."

Antonia blinked away her thoughts and met Lady MacKinnon's inquiring gaze.

"A letter just arrived for you."

Antonia knew who the letter's author would be. Since she'd taken the position as Lady MacKinnon's companion, her aunt was the only person who ever cared enough to write. The last note Antonia had received earlier in the year had not brought the best of news. Her father had yet to forgive her, and worse still, he had not asked her to return home.

She stared at the missive. *It must be more bad news.* A shiver of fear ran down her spine, sinking into the pit of her stomach.

"It is not going to open itself," Lady MacKinnon said with an impatient huff.

With trembling hands Antonia took the letter off the salver and prayed it was not the worst. She had only managed to read the first few sentences before tears began to stream down her face in a deluge.

"Oh, no. Is it bad new?" Lady MacKinnon questioned with concern.

Gulping down her tears, Antonia tried to maintain some form of dignity. "Yes, I'm afraid it is."

With hands clasped tightly, Lady MacKinnon leaned in and waited for her to continue.

"My father is ill," Antonia managed to sputter out, swallowing down hard on the lump in her throat. "It would seem he does… does not…" She gasped for air, unable to finish her sentence, then gave up trying to maintain her composure, and buried her face in her hands as grief consumed her.

"Oh, please don't cry, Mrs. Tomlin. You must go to him at once."

"But I don't…" she hiccupped on her sobs. It was a miserable time of year to embark on such a journey. Christmastide was only three weeks away, and the weather was unpredictable at best. The situation was hopeless—first her mother, now her father. Antonia had been foolish to run away from her problems. In doing so, she'd only created more.

"You will travel in my carriage." Lady MacKinnon's kind offer caught her off guard.

"But I couldn't possibly…"

"Nonsense," the older woman declared with a wave of her hand. "You will leave just as soon as the arrangements can be made."

Fear, regret, and appreciation mixed and collided in her stomach, creating an altogether odd combination. She was about to express her gratitude when Lady MacKinnon added, "And Mallory will accompany you."

There were very few people in the world Antonia did not like or get along with, and Lady MacKinnon's lady's maid was one of them. Mallory, although quite efficient in her duties, was—to put it simply—not a nice person. Antonia had always suspected that the maid had not believed her story when she first arrived at Castle MacKinnon nearly five years ago.

"I'm sure it is not necessary."

"Despite the fact you're a widow, you *are* still quite young, and exceptionally beautiful." Lady MacKinnon shook her head. "I will not have you traveling the length of Great Britain by yourself. It is not proper, and there is no one I trust more than Mallory."

Antonia knew better than to argue with her employer. Once Lady MacKinnon put her mind to something, the matter was settled. She would be travelling in Lady MacKinnon's carriage with the unwanted chaperone.

This was going to be a tedious journey.

♫♫♫

Since her aunt's letter arrived, Antonia had not had a moment's reprieve as she readied for the long journey south. She had not even allowed herself time to contemplate what it entailed. There would be time enough in the carriage to reflect on that. But one thing was for certain; despite everything that had happened, and all the hurtful words that had been spoken, Antonia had to see her father one last time.

Once her small trunk was packed and taken down to be stored for the hasty departure, she began setting aside the few remaining items to go in her traveling valise. No sooner had she began her task when Mallory entered her room in a rush of unpleasantness.

"I have been informed I'm to accompany you on the journey."

Antonia could hear the disdain in Mallory's voice, and it did not sit well with her. She would not be surprised if somewhere along the journey Mallory abandoned her and told their employer she had run off.

However, instead of arguing with the unpleasant woman, she tried a different tactic. "I know we have not often got on well, but I do appreciate your presence during this most challenging time." She thought she sounded more as if she were addressing Parliament than someone she was about to spend a great deal of time with, cooped up in a carriage for hours on end.

Mallory folded her hands neatly in front of her as she began her rebuke. "Do not use your sweet words with me. Why Lady MacKinnon ever felt sorry for you is beyond me. It is as plain as the nose on my face you have been lying from the moment you arrived here."

Antonia could feel her eyes widen with shock. Could Mallory truly know her secret? Raising her chin, she forced the words from her mouth. "I don't know whatever you mean, but since we will be traveling together, I do hope we can put whatever differences aside and, at the very least, be civil toward one another."

"Humph," Mallory breathed out in a harsh, high-pitched tone. "I do not intend to become friends with the likes of you." And with that final insult, the maid left the room.

Antonia shook her head and inwardly sighed. If Mallory only knew her true identity, perhaps she wouldn't treat her thusly. But she couldn't dwell on those thoughts when there were more pressing matters to contemplate. She began to pace the simple, sparsely decorated room, the swish of her widow's weeds adding to her growing anxiety.

What would happen once she arrived at her father's house? Would she be welcome? And what of her stepmother? Her once dearest friend, Hester, had a way of complicating her life. Not until it was too late had Antonia realized Hester only befriended her in order to become the next Lady Madeley. *That* betrayal still stung. No sooner had her father emerged from mourning for Antonia's dear mother, than he announced his engagement, and then married immediately by special license.

Antonia stopped her pacing. Her heart pounded against her chest like a runaway team of horses.

"Lord Trawden," she uttered on a whisper. "Dracon."

In all her worry over seeing her father, she'd completely forgotten about the possibility of seeing *him*. Her heart clamored with thoughts of her ex-fiancé. What if he discovered she'd returned? She hadn't even thought about that possibility. What was she going to do?

She had not felt this anxious since she had fled from Father's demands, and her engagement five years ago. *Damn*, but her fingers itched to hold her violin and run the bow over taut strings, to create music, to release the anxiety coursing through her veins. Among the dozens of things she missed and regretted, giving up her precious instrument was at the top of the list.

She couldn't dwell on past mistakes at present. She had more pressing matters plaguing her mind, namely how she was to survive the weeklong journey with Mallory.

CHAPTER 2

The journey had now dragged on for more than two weeks—weather, changing horses, and arrogant postilions adding to the delays. Christmastide was fast approaching, and Antonia had tired of Mallory's company—not to mention her constant complaining and excessive negativity—well over a week ago.

As they headed south, Antonia had plenty of time to reflect on her life up to that point. It had been a madcap scheme—one she'd regretted every day for the past five years. Her widow's weeds never ceased to remind her of her foolish behavior.

When she left, she thought she would at last be free to travel the world, but she had ended up more confined than ever. Pride—and perhaps a little stubbornness—had kept her from returning to her home. But now, she was tired of running away. Running from her father's demands. Running from a fiancé who had secrets of his own. Running from painful memories.

She rested her head against the seat's cushioned back. The opulence of Lady MacKinnon's carriage was another reminder of all that she had given up. She did not regret her time with Lady MacKinnon, and was thankful for the position, but it came at a heavy price.

She was the daughter of a baron, but had been reduced to being a paid companion with no prospects. Still, over the past years, she had learned a lot about herself and the kind of person she wanted to be. No longer concerned with elaborate gowns or preoccupied with the latest *on-dits*, she had learned to enjoy the simple, everyday pleasures life had to offer: early morning walks, pastel sunrises, and the sweet songs birds that greeted her with each new dawn.

The carriage lumbered along, slushing through mud, swaying back and forth in slow, heavy movements. "Oh, why won't this… this *thing* go any faster?" Mallory grumbled for what seemed like the hundredth time that day.

Although Antonia's sentiments secretly matched Mallory's, she was not about to engage in yet another unpleasant conversation. With each passing mile, the nervous energy that coursed through her body built, only finding some release through her tapping foot.

Mallory glared from across the dimly lit conveyance. "Mrs. Tomlin, would you please stop fidgeting?"

Antonia sucked in her reply. Throughout the arduous journey Mallory had scolded her about every little nuance, and complained to no end about… well, everything.

Not much longer now.

"Where in creation is your father's home?" Mallory's tone was none too pleasant. "And I suppose we will be trapped here until Twelfth Night." Her cold glare struck to the core of Antonia. "I do hope that the accommodations are satisfactory. Certainly not as grand as MacKinnon Castle, I presume," she said with a snicker.

Quite soon Mallory would discover the truth of Antonia's

heritage. Surely that would be when the maid would pack up her things and retreat to Lady MacKinnon to inform her that Antonia was not who she pretended to be. Then what? Antonia would have no position, no reference, no way to support herself.

She glanced out of the window, praying for a distraction from her thoughts. Dark, ominous clouds had begun to creep up, obscuring the sun. A lonely oak in the distance signaled they weren't far from Lionshead, the ancestral home of the man she was supposed to have married. She knew this stretch of land well; she had often explored in the meadow beyond as an adolescent.

Memories of a handsome couple picnicking in that meadow flooded her mind. It was the first time she had seen Lord Trawden with his new bride. They had appeared so happy and in love. That fairytale dream had become Antonia's solemn promise to herself. But those schoolgirl dreams had been tarnished and shattered beneath the weight of death, rumors, and her mother's confession. And like her hopes, Lord and Lady Trawden's fairytale had not lasted.

Running away had not solved any of Antonia's problems or eased her fears. If anything, over the years, they had grown. But somewhere in the past hundred miles she had decided the moment had come for her to face the music. Her father was ill, and she had little time left with him. She had to put her feelings for her stepmother aside and cherish what little Father had left to give. She prayed she was not too late.

The carriage jerked to the right, then sharply to the left, halting her musings. The howling wind pressed them forward. The hour wasn't too late, but by now, the clouds had turned day to night. Antonia grabbed the hand strap as the carriage continued to sway round the bend. She glanced out the window. The road leading to the village veered off to the left, and in the distance, the faint glow of civilization could be seen.

Thunder drummed overhead, reverberating through the carriage. Antonia clenched her teeth tight and prayed the storm would pass quickly. Her hand was beginning to ache from clutching the strap so tightly. A warning voice whispered in her head. Something did not feel right. She didn't know what it was, but perhaps being this close to Lionshead and having to pass *his* home was what had set her nerves on edge. Whatever it was, she wished she could will it to stop.

She continued to jiggle her leg and tap her free hand. Nothing was relieving the tension that twisted her insides tighter and tighter, like the string of her violin being wound too tight and ready to snap at any moment.

Mallory huffed out a loud, annoyed breath. "I do wish you would…"

The carriage rocked sharply to the right. A loud crack broke through the sounds of the countryside, then horses neighing, men yelling, and above it all, Mallory's intense shriek echoed around her. She was flung to the opposite end of the seat, slamming hard into the wall. Scrambling to clutch the hand strap, she struggled to stay upright. The carriage shifted to one side, teetering for a moment. She held her breath. *I don't want to die.* But as if ignoring her silent plea, the vehicle tipped, rolling over and over.

Fracturing wood cracking, screams, and cries pierced her ears. The noise crescendoed to deafening proportions. Fear crept up her throat. *I don't want to die.*

Through the chaos, she offered a silent prayer. *Please let me live. I will make amends. Please…* She chanted the words over and over until all that was left was deathly silence.

CHAPTER 3

The frigid wind slapping against Dracon's face was far more annoying than the heavy deluge of rain that was trying to saturate his clothes. The road was deserted. No one with an ounce of common sense would dare be out on such a miserable night. He should have been home by now, but the wind and rain had slowed his progress. Thuban was a strong horse, but even he was showing signs of fatigue.

A fork in the road signaled that he was almost home. To the left lay the tiny village and to the right, Lionshead.

For a brief moment, he thought about taking a detour and staying the night at the local inn. At least then he would not have to pass the churchyard. He detested *that* church. A deep agony mixed with anger still coursed through his veins. He had been living with the guilt that he'd been unable to save them for such a long time that he couldn't remember a time without it.

He shook those thoughts away and focused on the lonely road that led to an even lonelier house filled with too many painful memories—a house that had not witnessed joy in over ten years. There had been a brief chance at happiness, but it had slipped between his large fingers and fled to Gretna Green. But despite the years, he was still in love with her.

"Not long now." He rubbed Thuban's neck, encouraging him on. Even at this slow pace, they should reach Lionshead within the hour.

A hazy mist slanted against the landscape, sending a strange eeriness rapping along his spine. In the dreary distance he spied an odd shape half hanging over the embankment. He squinted until the dark object came into focus.

"Damn," he swore into the twilight, his breath puffing in front of him in a billowy, ghost-like cloud. He kicked Thuban into a gallop.

After what felt like dozens of minutes later, he finally reached the mangled carriage, dismounted, and started pulling through the wreckage for survivors. He did not have to take a second look closer to know that the two bodies crushed beneath the weight of the conveyance had both perished. One of the horses lay dead off to the side. He climbed on top of the wreckage and opened the now upward-facing door. Peering inside, he saw two figures. He pulled the already damaged side panel away from the carriage, giving further access to the occupants inside. Leaning over the first female, he felt for a pulse. Nothing.

A moan came from the opposite corner. He edged closer. Rain from the open door above trickled in. All was silent for a brief moment before the cracking of wood rose in a steady crescendo.

There was no time to lose.

Without further thought, he kicked out what was left of the side panel, scooped the injured woman into his arms, and slid out of the debris. Seconds later, the carriage shifted further on its side and plunged into the ditch. The sound of splintering echoed through the stillness.

Carrying the woman to a nearby tree, he eased her onto the ground. She was clad in black, her damp hair covering most of her face. A slight, painful moan escaped her lips.

"Shh, I mean you no harm. There was an accident." He began smoothing her dark, wet hair away from her blood-stained cheek. "I…" The words caught in his throat as soft green eyes met his for a second before fluttering shut.

Antonia.

Five years of solitude that had numbed his soul shattered at the sight of her. Those years of regret rushed through his heart, and pent-up longing dissipated in a single breath. He looked up at the fierce dark clouds overhead and swore on all that was holy, that as long as there was breath in his body, he was not going to lose her. Not again.

With each beat of his stuttering heart, worry kicked at him. What the hell was she doing out on a night like this? Why were they even traveling at night? Why had they not stopped at the inn?

Antonia's body shivered, centering his thoughts on her. Now was not the time to discern the meaning of all this. He took off his overcoat and covered her, then went to retrieve Thuban. At this hour, the chance of another passerby was slim. He had no choice but to take her to Lionshead on horse-back. He would send his stablemen to deal with the deceased and the wrecked carriage.

Carefully draping Antonia over Thuban's back, Dracon quickly mounted. He brought her cold, limp body gently into his embrace, cradling her against his chest, hoping to bring her some warmth.

The spicy scent of carnation surrounded him, reminding him again of wasted years. Disquietude over the past gave way to relief. She was alive, in his arms, *and* wearing widow's weeds. "Please let her live. Please give us another chance," he murmured into the darkness. Lightning barreled across the sky as if to answer his plea.

With the rain pounding down upon them, it seemed to take hours to reach Lionshead. As they neared the drive, the storm eased a little, and Dracon quickened their pace. Antonia was now a flame in his arms as fever began to consume her. Dread knotted his insides, and he growled up to the sky, "Damn it, let her live."

The moment he reached the circular drive, the front door flew open. Shouts and chaos ensued as he issued orders while carrying Antonia into the house.

"Ready the white suite!" He bellowed his order to no one in particular, but knew it would be done.

He took the stairs two at a time, not caring if the staff gawked at the lack of propriety. Bess, the housekeeper, was waiting for him. "This way, my lord."

He eased Antonia on the bed and looked down at her torn, muddy attire. His heart lurched with thoughts of what was supposed to be, but never was. He should be angry with her, but all he felt was a desire to protect her, to make things right.

"Get her out of those drenched garments. I will return shortly."

After servants were dispatched, Dracon changed out of his own soaked clothing, then rushed to Antonia's room. His body screamed for rest after such a long journey, but sleep would have to wait. There were too many emotions playing in his mind. He wanted nothing more than to believe that she had come back to him, but he guessed the more likely reason was she had ventured here to visit her father, Lord Madeley.

Lord Madeley and Dracon had been friends, but after Antonia fled the day before their wedding, their friendship had come to an end. There had been no reasoning with Lord Madeley. He had blamed Dracon for Antonia's flight and hadn't spoken to him since. The new Lady Madeley was the most likely culprit for that decision. She had been stirring all sorts of trouble with her incessant gossip for quite some time.

As Dracon entered the white suite, he couldn't help but recall the day he'd given the order to have these rooms renovated for Antonia, and the adjoining one for himself. For one brief moment, he'd had happiness within his grasp.

He crept closer to the bed, fear gripping his heart as he saw Antonia's motionless form. She could not die. He would not let her die. He—no, they both, deserved a second chance at happiness.

"Is the fever gone?" he said, startling the housekeeper.

Bess looked over her shoulder and glanced up at him. The dire look consuming her features darkened his mood. "No, it has worsened."

"Send for Osanna. Make sure she brings her satchel of herbs." If anyone could save Antonia, it would be the mystic. "I will sit with Antonia."

Bess gathered Antonia's soiled clothing and walked toward him. "Try not to worry, my lord. And think about getting some rest."

How could he not worry? This was Antonia, *his* Antonia. He dismissed Bess' words and pulled a large chair to the bedside. The dirt and blood had been wiped away from Antonia's face, revealing delicate cheek bones, a dainty nose, and delectable bow-shaped lips. Bess had dressed her in a white night rail, surely from her belongings that had been brought here a couple of days before they were due to marry. Even after all these years, he hadn't had the heart to part with them.

He stared down at her features. Streaks of gold danced through her brown hair. She was even lovelier than he remembered. But despite her ethereal appearance, she was red with fever, and a large gash on her forehead added to his fears. He took the cloth from the nightstand, dipped it into the water basin, then squeezed out the water, before wiping her forehead.

His heart ached and constricted as a feeling of helplessness consumed him. He didn't know what to do to save her. Brushing a kiss across her inflamed forehead, he whispered, "I will take care of you."

Hours later, he was still in that same position when Osanna came and administered the herbs. Even after the mystic had gone, he remained at Antonia's side. Darkness turned to light as a new day dawned, but she was still feverish. At some point during that day, Bess insisted that he leave the room and rest. He managed to stay away for one long, painful hour.

As he watched Antonia's features shift from calm to painful agony, fear—stark and vivid—coursed through him. He rubbed the back of his neck as helplessness continued to tighten and strangle his insides. He brushed damp locks of hair from her face. A hoarse gasp left her mouth, and she mumbled indiscernible words, and tears streamed down her face, mingling with sweat as she thrashed from side to side, trapped in a nightmare, wrestling with unseen ghosts.

He wanted to ease her pain, to comfort her. Without further thought, he scooped her up and carried her toward the roaring fire. Keeping her nestled within his embrace, he sat and rocked her petite form.

"Shh, I won't let anything happen to you." Unrestrained words fell from his mouth. "You have to live. I won't let you die. I can't lose you again, *my Antonia*."

Mere days ago, before he had left London, his sister had felt obligated to remind him that Christmastide was supposed to be a joyous time of year, one for new beginnings. But instead of finding joy, he was watching over his beloved, waiting for death to snatch away the once bright light in his life. Only he was not going to let death win, not again.

As night encroached upon the land and the storm continued to beat down on the already sodden countryside, Dracon continued to keep vigil and pray that, at any moment, Antonia would wake. Although her fever had broken, and she seemed to be resting peacefully, she had yet to awaken.

Shadows danced across the walls, fueled by firelight. He rubbed his face and tired eyes. His memory drifted to the past, to the memory of his first wife, and all he had lost.

As he stared into the flames, that tragic night, ingrained forever in his memory, played out with painful clarity. Images of Catherine running down the stairs in a flurry of excitement, her giddy laughter filling the hall, still haunted his nights. "I felt the baby," she had exclaimed with such joy. He could still see her even now and remembered thinking how vibrant she looked. And for one brief moment his world had seemed complete until she lost her footing, and tumbled down the stairs. Laughter had turned to terrified screams, then all was silent. He'd raced to her side, but he was too late.

Servants had come running from all corners of the house, only to find him kneeling beside her lifeless body. Rumors swirled that he had killed his wife, and the hushed murmurs of polite society had left him all but ostracized. A solitary man, he had suffered in silence for five long years until his troubled soul was touched by the sound of a single violin.

He rubbed his hand across his face once more. Fatigue was rapidly claiming him.

"My lord, it has been two days. You need rest." Bess' kind voice brought him back to the living. "Go and rest. I will sit with her."

"No," he uttered gravely, hardly recognizing his own

voice. "I will not leave her side," he growled. "I will not let her die."

"Sitting here is not going to change whatever Fate has in store."

Aside from his sister, Bess was the only other person who dared to speak her mind to him. She had been with his family since he was an infant, and had always nurtured and cared for him and his siblings as if they were her own. He did not take orders from anyone, but Bess had always had the ability to make him change his mind.

She placed a gentle hand on his arm. "Brooding is not going to help her. At the very least go and change. Barnelby has readied your things."

With great reluctance, he left the room.

♫♫♫

LAVENDER WAFTED THROUGH THE AIR, awakening Antonia's senses. Her eyes fluttered open. Through heavy lids, she saw muted sunlight streaking into the room. The sound of light rain tapping on the glass had a painful staccato dancing inside her sore head. Without moving her aching body, she glanced about the elegant white room, her gaze settling on the painting overhead. Four chubby putti, each playing a violin, returned her scrutiny with a smile. A garland of pink roses framed the heavenly musical quartet, and behind them, a lush green landscape and a crisp blue sky faded into the distance. It was as if the picture had been created just for her.

Where was she? The last thing she remembered was the carriage swerving out of control. Screams and cries echoed in her mind. Where was Mallory?

A soft, masculine moan startled her. She bolted upright,

only to regret the hasty decision. Closing her eyes, she gripped her head and took in several deep breaths.

"Shh." A warm hand caressed her shoulder. "You have a couple of bumps and a nasty gash on your head," a familiar husky voice soothed.

She tried to open her eyes, but the pain was blinding. She clamped her eyes shut, begging the throbbing to ease. His warm hand slid off her shoulder, then she heard him step away.

"Where am I?" she whispered with a dry rasp.

There was a long silence, and the room seemed to darken. A moment later, she felt his presence beside her again.

"You're at Lionshead, Antonia."

CHAPTER 4

Lionshead... Dracon.

Antonia tilted her head toward the sound of his voice and forced her lids to open a sliver. Piercing blue eyes gazed down on her, not with hatred or anger as she expected after what she had done, but with a caring gentleness that made her heart lurch. Why did he still have an effect on her after all this time?

Remember what Mother said, her mind offered the somber reminder.

Dracon eased her back on the pillow and pulled the blanket up over her chest. "Do you recall what happened?" His tone was just as caring and gentle as the look in his eyes.

Memories of the last moments before the carriage rocked violently came flooding back into her mind. She remembered looking out of the window as the weak light was just beginning to fade into the horizon. The rain had delayed them, and thunder had angrily rolled overhead. A loud crack followed by screams careened through her memory—and then...

"What happened to...?"

His forlorn face told her that no one else had survived.

"Oh." Mallory had not been her favorite person, but nonetheless, she had never wished the woman any harm, despite her unpleasantness and hurtful intentions.

"Why were you traveling at night?"

Antonia struggled to remember all the events leading up to the accident. "We had been delayed by our postilion and last change of horses. Mallory was furious and insisted the driver make up for lost time."

"Mallory?"

"Yes, my…" Her head began to pound anew. She closed her eyes, trying to focus on her words. "… traveling companion," she muttered. She brought her hand up to rub her temples, but touched a large and rather sensitive bump on her head. "Ooh." She sucked in her breath.

Dracon eased her hand away, replacing it with a lavender-scented wet cloth.

"How… how long have I been here?" she managed to ask through the piercing pain in her head.

"Four days."

Four days? Her mind was reeling. What of her father? Through the sharp ringing in her ears, she heard Dracon speaking but could not discern his words. The pain in her head had grown to epic proportions. She kept her eyes closed, attempting to relax, hoping to feel some relief.

After several deep breaths, the pounding began to ease to a slow pianissimo, and Dracon's concerned voice reached her. "Osanna has been summoned and will administer more herbs. I will let you rest now."

"Thank you," she whispered.

When she woke next, the room was dark and hidden in shadows. She stretched her aching limbs, wondering how long she had been asleep this time. Although her body remained sore, the throbbing pain in her head had subsided to a dull ache. A faint orange glow from the fireplace drew her gaze, and then the large wingback chair, halfway between the fireplace and her bed—and partially shadowed, caught her attention. She blinked several times, trying to focus, when she realized Dracon was sitting in the chair.

Her pounding heart disrupted all other sounds. Had he watched over her the entire time? Why was he being so caring? Why had he not just sent her home? Dozens of questions demanded answers, but her head protested. She eased back down on the pillow, assuring herself that she would discover the answers in due time.

♪♪♪

EXHAUSTED FROM KEEPING vigil by Antonia's side for the fourth night in a row, Dracon trudged toward his study, hoping to accomplish some of the estate business that had piled up while he'd been away.

He entered the warm space, thankful the fire had already been lit and was doing its job. Slumping into the soft leather desk chair, he pulled one of several stacks of papers and a ledger nearer and attempted to work.

He stared at the lines and columns, but no matter how hard he tried, thoughts of Antonia kept creeping into his mind. Images of her playing the violin had often taunted him over the past five years, and now that she was at Lionshead, he wanted almost nothing more than to hear her play again.

Slamming the ledger closed, he pushed away from the desk and went to the window. The weather had improved slightly; patches of blue sky had managed to break through the grey clouds. Staring out at the saturated landscape, his mind drifted to the first time he had heard her playing.

He had not wanted to attend Lady Rede's summer musicale, but he knew his late wife's aunt would not accept him declining her invitation. The white gazebo was decorated for the festivities with garlands of greenery and sprigs of carnations that burst with color.

He suffered through an hour of talentless ladies and was about to take his leave when the sight of Antonia halted his departure. She was like an angel sent from above, dressed in celestial blue. With violin in hand, she walked up the steps, the look on her face one of sheer terror. The bow in her hand shook as she prepared to play, but the moment it touched the strings she came to life—and Dracon did the same. It was as if a part of him had been dormant. She played with such conviction, such passion, that he was mesmerized.

Hours later, he managed to steal a moment alone with her, and his praise and compliments brought a blush to her cheeks. Her sweet shyness and humble nature only added to the intense feelings her music had stirred in him.

For the next few months, he attempted to coax her out of her shyness, but she remained unsure of him. When Lord Madeley approached him, offering his daughter's hand in marriage, Dracon thought he had found his second chance at love.

"Pardon me, Lord Trawden," Fulbert said after clearing his throat, breaking through Dracon's thoughts. "Miss Rede is waiting in the drawing room."

Dracon rolled his eyes heavenward. *Grant me patience.* He nodded in response, then proceeded reluctantly downstairs.

Miss Rede was his late wife's cousin and a constant thorn in his side. Within a day or two of returning to Lionshead, Miss Rede never failed to darken his doorstep. He suspected she was interested in becoming the next Lady Trawden, but he was most certainly not interested in that proposition.

The air cooled as he made his way down. The ground floor was rarely used and never heated, and the drawing room was not Dracon's favorite room as the heavy, mahogany furniture and somber tapestries reminded him of his late father—the most distant and uncaring man if there ever was one.

The moment Dracon entered the dark space and saw Miss Rede's cheerful smile, he knew it would be difficult to escape. Seconds later, his assumption was confirmed.

"Lord Trawden, I cannot tell you how pleased I was to hear you have returned to Lionshead for Christmastide. Mother insists that you join us for Christmas dinner, and of course, the annual masquerade and Twelfth Night party."

With his usual stoic tone in place, he interjected, "Thank you for the invitation, but I will not be venturing from Lionshead."

Miss Rede drew her brows together. "Why ever not? Surely you do not want to be alone…" Her words trailed off as she received the harsh glare he cast her way. "What I meant to say was," she began again as she stepped closer to him, her voice turning silky. "I am concerned. I cannot bear the thought of you being alone during the festive season."

Dracon had always detested women who tried to use their feminine wiles on him. It had not worked in the past, and it would not work now.

"I will not be alone."

"Oh." Disappointment flickered across her features.

"Now if you will excuse me."

He started to take his leave, but before he could take even one step, Miss Rede unleashed a flurry of questions and statements meant to draw out her stay. "Did you hear about the terrible carriage accident? Mama heard that there were no survivors. Such a tragedy and so close to Christmas. I wonder who the occupants were?"

He weighed his options. It would be common knowledge soon enough that Antonia had returned and was convalescing at Lionshead. This was the countryside, after all, and few secrets could be kept here longer than a fortnight. Better to state the facts rather than have rumors fly.

"There was one survivor."

"Oh?" Her ears perked with interest.

"Miss Madeley," he said, using Antonia's maiden name. He would not acknowledge her elopement and subsequent widowhood, at least not to Miss Rede.

"Antonia is here?" The sound of utter disbelief rang through her words. "I did not think she would ever return, not since…" She cleared her throat. "I haven't seen her in such a long time. I would love to spend the afternoon…"

"She is convalescing." He used his most firm, no-nonsense tone, hoping she would take the hint.

Miss Rede pressed, "Why has she not returned to Madeley Hall?"

Clearly hints were too subtle for the likes of Miss Rede. He'd had enough of this conversation. "If you will excuse me, I have estate business that requires my attention." He was not going to wait to hear the further barrage of questions that would certainly be forthcoming. He simply turned and walked out of the room. He could only hope Miss Rede *would* take offense and decide to never call on him again.

Instead of returning to his study, he wandered the halls, trying to gather the courage to see Antonia. He was never intimidated by anyone else, and yet, for some odd reason, his nerves—and words—always seemed to fail him whenever he was near her.

While Antonia was unconscious and feverish, he had not left her side. But the moment she'd awoken, he'd kept his distance, waiting for her to heal. There would be time enough to discuss the past. The reasons why she had run away were still unknown to him, although he had his suspicions. Even after ten years, gossip still swirled around Catherine's death. How could anyone believe he had murdered his wife?

Although he was not in any hurry to send Antonia back to Madeley Hall, he knew his time with her was short, and there was still so much to learn. He'd sent word to her father the moment the weather had cleared, and received a response just that morning that Lord and Lady Madeley were not in residence. However, they were due to return just before Christmastide, barring no weather delays.

Dracon paced the length of the long gallery for the umpteenth time. He had been inquiring after Antonia's health every couple of hours, each time hoping for better news. But his attempt at patience was wearing as thin as the rug beneath his aching feet.

The soft sound of footsteps halted his pace. He turned around and met Osanna's dark, caring eyes. "How is she?" he asked.

"The gash on her forehead is healing quite nicely, but the two bumps on her head are causing her much discomfort. She needs to rest, but she is young and far too restless to stay put for so long."

"Thank you for keeping me abreast."

Osanna departed, leaving him to continue his pacing.

What could he offer? What would soothe… An idea struck.

He rushed to the chilly, dark marquess' suite. He had not used these rooms for a very long time, not since… He brushed those thoughts away. These rooms still held too many painful memories.

Strolling to the large armoire, he gripped the handle as he took in a deep breath. A carved lion's head stared down at him from the pediment. Releasing his breath, he opened one of the heavy doors. He stared at the column of drawers for a just a moment, hoping, praying this was the right decision. Reaching for the top drawer, he pulled on the warped wood until it freed. It had been five years since he'd viewed the items he'd locked away in this armoire. He withdrew a dark green velvet pouch, undid the tie, and pulled a small wooden box from its velvety cocoon.

The lid was encrusted with a dragon and lion set against a royal blue background. His family crest was a reminder of how he had failed in his duties. He brushed his hand across the emblem, then lifted the lid. A delicate song drifted from the music box, striking his heart. Hopeful memories of a bygone time teased the corner of his mind. It was as if not a day had gone by.

Antonia had always loved music. This little music box had been meant to be a gift for his new bride, but that joyous day had never come. So, it had been locked up, collecting dust, just like his heart.

He hesitated for a moment. Regardless of the past, he wanted Antonia to have it. It would be the first step toward making amends.

CHAPTER 5

*A*ntonia stared up at the ceiling, focusing on the cherubs overhead. She was still unsure of all that had happened. She knew that she was at Lionshead, but was confused as to why Dracon had been keeping his distance, especially since she felt certain he had remained at her bedside through the long hours when fever had disturbed her dreams and turned them into perfect nightmares. Nightmares about her mother dying. Nightmares about her father's lack of caring. Nightmares about her own selfish actions.

Would the pain of the past ever fade?

Hot tears stung the corners of her eyes. She turned on her side to wipe away the moisture on her pillow when she noticed a small, emerald-green velvet pouch on the nightstand. She propped herself up, then reached for it, the soft, rich material playing against her fingers. She opened the sack and pulled out a small box. Instantly, she recognized Dracon's family crest. She lifted the lid and was rewarded with the cheerful, crystalline sound of a simple melody.

Intense longing pummeled her heart, bringing more hot tears to her eyes. Why was Dracon being so kind to her after all she had done? If only she had been honest, perhaps they could have been happy together, but now…

She placed the trinket box on the nightstand and eased back down onto the pillow. Looking up at the quartet of putti, her mind drifted to the first time she had met Dracon. She had always thought him handsome, but when he had complimented her on playing the violin, it was as if he understood her passion. Something deeper had touched her heart. She had never felt that way before, not then, and not since.

She knew now she had been wrong to run away, but at the time, the prospect of marrying her father's choice, a man who was clearly still in love with his dead wife, had been too much to bear. And Dracon's deference to all things Catherine had crushed her heart. On the few occasions she had visited Lionshead, haunting images of Lady Trawden's tragic accident had tormented her imagination. Combined with her mother's deathbed confession—"Your father never loved me the way he loved his first wife. I always lived in her shadow"—was more than Antonia could tolerate. She had not been able to shake the certainty that had she married Dracon, she would have ended up like her mother: alone, addicted to laudanum, and waiting for death to relieve her broken heart.

"I see you are feeling better." Bess' cheerful voice was a welcome distraction to her brooding thoughts.

"I am. Thank you." She had been too weak to venture out, but was feeling better today and hoped to leave her room soon. Although she was thankful for the constant company Bess provided, she was tired of being cooped up, alone with her thoughts.

"What shall we discuss today?"

Antonia brought her knees to her chin and rested her cheek against them. A question sprung from her mouth without thought. "What was Lord Trawden like as a child?"

Although they had been engaged, she really did not know him. She knew how he appeared on the outside—tall, with a handsome countenance that held piercing blue eyes—but she was curious about the man behind the stoic façade. She suspected Dracon had learned to hide his feelings after his first wife's tragic demise, but she had glimpsed a certain passion when he talked about Antonia's violin playing. She wanted to know *that* man.

"Well, he never got into trouble, but his sister, on the other hand—" Bess let out a long whistle. "That one was always getting into trouble, whether it be climbing trees in her finest dress, or getting all muddy. Poor Lord Trawden, he was the one who came to her rescue, usually getting more than he bargained for in the process."

Antonia's laughter filled the room, and it felt wonderful. She couldn't remember the last time she'd truly laughed. It was as if suddenly something had freed inside of her. She'd been unhappy for so long, brooding over the past. Life may not be perfect, or the one she'd dreamed of—she didn't know what tomorrow or the next day would bring—but in that moment, she made up her mind to find snippets of happiness each day.

"What false tales of mischief has Bess been weaving?" Dracon's deep voice broke through the laughter, causing Antonia's heart to skip a beat, but not in fear. Something deep down stirred, and she realized that she'd missed him and was delighted that he had come to visit her.

"That's between Bess and me," she teased.

His lovely blue eyes assessed her, which roused even more tingles, and then he spoke, "And how is our patient today?" His concern sent warmth rippling through her.

She could feel the heat rising in her cheeks, but before she could respond, Bess spoke up. "Much better. It won't be long before she can travel to Madeley Hall."

Perhaps Antonia was mistaken, but she thought she saw a look of disappointment pass over Dracon's features before hidden behind the stoic façade. *Wishful thinking*, she sighed inwardly. Despite how her body reacted, and her heart hoped, deep down, she knew he was just being kind. He had always had a strong sense of duty.

Dracon stepped further into the room but stood several feet from the bed. He eyed her with a quiet contemplation. It used to bother her the way he would watch her, but now... she wanted him to see her.

Damn, why did he have this effect on her?

"Oh, dear me, but the water in the teapot is cold. I will fetch a fresh pot." And with that, Bess left the room, leaving Antonia and Dracon alone.

She watched as his features changed. Was it her imagination, or did he appear as nervous as she felt? The battering her head had suffered must be clouding her mind. There was no other explanation for her contradictory thoughts or foreign sensations building within.

Pushing those impossible dreams aside, she decided to broach the subject of her father's ill health. Although she desperately wanted to see her papa, she was not well enough to travel yet. She prayed that he was still well. The thought of losing another parent so close to Christmas was too much to even contemplate.

She worried the edge of the blanket for several seconds before mustering the courage to speak. "I...I was wondering if you sent word to... to my father." She swallowed the hard lump in her throat as fear over her father's ill health took hold of her imagination.

Dracon's deep voice was a soothing balm to her nerves.

"Once the weather cleared, I sent a letter to Madeley Hall. I was informed this morning that Lord and Lady Madeley, along with your aunt, are in Bath and are due to return before Christmas Eve."

"Bath?" Perhaps Antonia had misunderstood her aunt's letter, and her father was taking the waters at Bath as a last resort.

He raised a curious brow. "Yes, I believe the weather is more temperate in Bath this time of year than here."

"Yes, of course." She tried to hide her worries and confusion. Her aunt's letter had seemed most dire, and yet her father had travelled far from home.

Dracon cleared his throat as he rubbed the back of his neck. He looked like an uncertain little boy asking for a special treat. "I hope you are not opposed to continuing convalescing at Lionshead while awaiting your father's return."

She was enjoying seeing this side of him—not quite relaxed, but certainly not intimidating. "Not at all," she said as she offered a smile. "Thank you for allowing me to stay here."

He returned the smile, and quickly added, "I have also taken the liberty of arranging a wardrobe for you since all your belongings were destroyed in the accident."

She did not know what to say. Dracon had seen to all her needs without so much as a single word from her. Guilt settled in the pit of her stomach like a brick. After all she had done, he was still gracious as ever.

He strolled to the fireplace and stared for long moments into the flames. Inhaling deeply, he turned around and blurted out, "I would greatly enjoy your company tonight at dinner. If you feel you can manage it."

She nodded her head in acceptance. He offered a quick smile before abruptly turning to take his leave.

"Thank you for the music box," she called, desperate for him to stay a little longer. "It is quite lovely."

He halted and glanced back at her. Her words seemed to have surprised him. "You are welcome, Antonia."

♪♪♪

ANTONIA SAT at the dressing table readying for dinner. A nervous excitement swept through her. Wanting to look perfect this evening—well, as perfect as she could under the circumstances—she pulled a crimson ribbon from the drawer and attempted to pull her hair back into an acceptable style. A sharp pounding at her temples halted her efforts.

She ran a gentle finger over the larger of the two bumps on her head. It was still sensitive to the touch but had greatly reduced in size. The gash wasn't as bad as she first had thought and had already begun to heal. Osanna had prescribed a concoction of herbs to help reduce scarring. Antonia was not really concerned with the appearance of it, but both Bess and Osanna had insisted on the balm.

"My hair will have to remain down," she sighed to her reflection, not entirely displeased with the option. Her vanity had always been her long wavy hair. She thought it her nicest feature and would spend an hour each evening brushing her long locks.

After taking one last glance in the mirror, she gathered her crimson shawl and headed toward the salon. As she walked down the hall, taking in the family portraits, she could not help but think of Dracon's first wife.

Years ago, Miss Rede had revealed how much her cousin

had loved Lionshead, and painstakingly decorated the house upon her marriage to Lord Trawden. Everywhere Antonia turned, she could not escape the ghost of Catherine, the beloved first wife. A shiver ran through her body, settling into an uneasy fist in her stomach. No matter how much she cared for Dracon, it would never be enough. He was still in love with his first wife, of that much she remained sure, and, in this, she had not changed her mind; she did not want to be second to a deceased woman's memory.

By the time she entered the salon, she was not feeling herself. Her head was aching once more, and her stomach was in knots.

"Are you unwell?" Dracon's deep voice reached her ears before she even realized he was in the room.

"My head is still sensitive." She did not want to reveal what else was bothering her. "I apologize for my appearance." She ran her hand down a long lock of hair. "It is quite uncomfortable for my hair to be up."

"No need to apologize." Dracon's gaze settled on her hand as he cleared his throat. "You have beautiful hair."

Her pulse began to beat erratically, and not in an unpleasant way. *He's just being kind, you ninny.* "I…I wanted to thank you for rescuing me and…" She could not manage to formulate her words into a cohesive sentence.

His gaze was a soft caress that sent her insides fluttering. "You have no need to thank me. I am relieved that you are here."

All thoughts of her sore head faded as the warmth of his smile sent her pulse racing anew. Dracon took a step closer. "Antonia…"

"Dinner is served, Lord Trawden," Fulbert, Lionshead's aged butler announced as he entered the salon, breaking the spell.

"Shall we?" Dracon offered her his arm.

She prayed he could not hear the hammering of her heart as she took his offered arm. Something seemed to have shifted between them. Or was it just her imagination? Or more likely, hope. Confusion laced her thoughts, muddling reality.

He escorted her in the opposite direction, away from the dining room. "Since it is only the two of us, I thought an informal dinner in the white parlor would be more comfortable."

With each passing moment, her feelings toward him were becoming more topsy-turvy. Since her arrival, he had been nothing but kind and sincere in all his actions, and yet, the past—especially his past—kept strangling her thoughts, not letting her nerves ease.

"Do you still play the violin?"

He remembered that she played?

She looked away, too humiliated to look him in the eye. "No," she whispered, hoping that he would not pry.

After she ran away, dreams of traveling and seeing the world were quickly halted when she realized she had not the funds to survive beyond a fortnight. In an act of desperation, she sold her most prized possession, her violin. It was one of the worst days of her life. That was one confession she was not willing to share. Changing the subject was imperative.

"This room is quite lovely," she said as they walked into the white parlor. She glanced about the opulent space. Gone were the dark and somber colors she remembered from her last visit, replaced with white panels and intricate details in gold leaf. Soft moonlight cascaded in through the gothic windows. The dancing putti around the cornice brought a smile to her face. She sat in the offered chair, still glancing about in amazement. "So beautiful," she said on a sigh.

"My sister believes it rather stark," he said with a chuckle. "Not enough color in her estimation."

"Oh no, I think all white is wonderful. It reminds me of snow and wintertime."

"A time when the world lay dormant, waiting for spring, but even in its sleepy state, it stirs the imagination." His poetic words touched her heart.

"That is quite a lovely sentiment," she said as she met his smoldering gaze.

For a long moment, everything around them stilled. With each breath she took, her feelings for him intensified. Ever since she'd first spied him all those years ago when she was a young girl, she'd fancied herself half in love with him. She was beginning to think her infatuation had grown.

Glancing away, she admired the elaborate spread before them. The smell of roasted meat and vegetables made her mouth water. "There is quite a bit of food for just the two of us."

"It would appear that Cook does not want you to go hungry," he teased affectionately.

For the next hour, the conversation during the meal was light and pleasant. He shared some childhood memories of bygone Christmas and Twelfth Night celebrations. She was enjoying this relaxed side of him. He was most attentive and seemed intent on putting her at ease as he served a veritable feast of roasted beef, buttered peas, and *ragoût à la Française*. By the time the dessert course was laid, she doubted she would be able to take another bite.

"Would you care for a sherry?"

"That would be lovely, thank you." As he began to slowly pour the glass of wine, he watched her out of the corner of his eye. Desperate to ease the rush of tingles, she said the first thing that came to mind. "I was wondering about the lovely *trompe l'oeil* in my room."

He stopped mid-pour, his hand shaking ever so slightly. Several droplets of rich amber liquid fell, staining the white tablecloth. He looked away, suddenly interested in the decanter. He cleared his throat and almost shyly responded, "I had it done for you."

"Me?"

He took in a long, deep breath before he spoke again. "I knew how much you loved playing the violin, and since those rooms weren't being used…" His words died as the heat of his stare bore down on her. Then he retreated behind a stoic mask that revealed no more of what he was thinking, but she was certain that it had to do with his first wife. The food that she had been enjoying only moments ago turned sour in her stomach.

The ghosts of the past twisted and strangled the joy she'd been experiencing. Her heart ached for his loss, and for what could never be.

CHAPTER 6

*I*n the span of a minute, the enjoyable evening Dracon was sharing with Antonia came to an end. He thought she would have been pleased to know that he'd had the trompe l'oeil painted especially for her, but her reaction was far from what he'd expected. Something more than her injuries was troubling her. He wished she would confide in him.

"Would you mind if I retired, my head…" she said as she raised her long delicate fingers to her brow. Those wonderful fingers that had coaxed magic out of her violin. How he longed to watch her play, to hear her music, and feel it in his soul.

"Not at all." He forced the words. He didn't know what else to say. Somehow, he had made a mess of the situation.

He stood and watched her stroll from the room without another word. The elegant sway of her hips entranced him, stirring long-denied desires. He forced those fantasies away and sat back down, taking the glass of wine in hand. Swirling the deep burgundy liquid, his mind strayed to this new conundrum.

He was puzzled why she no longer played the violin. He'd wanted to pursue the reason, but the sadness evident in her lovely green eyes had begged him not to.

Damn, but he was an insensitive ass. Of course, she was upset. Clearly, she had lost everything in the accident.

He pushed away from the table, almost tipping the chair over. For the second time since Antonia had arrived, he found himself venturing toward the marquess' suite to retrieve something he had locked away many years ago. He found a small metal key with an elaborate decoration on the bow in his bureau, then, opening the armoire doors, he unlocked the deep bottom drawer. An elegant oblong case beckoned, but it would have to wait. He was only the benefactor.

♪♪♪

LAST NIGHT, Dracon's question about playing the violin had disturbed her thoughts and tormented her dreams. It had been such a long time since she had played, and she missed her beloved instrument. It had been a source of comfort, a means to come alive, and its absence had caused her much grief.

She walked the length of the room, strolling to the window to gaze out on the morning landscape. She laid her hand on the glass and felt coolness emanate from it. However, it did not sooth the burning ache she felt in her fingers.

A soft knock sounded, followed by Bess' cheery voice. "Good morning, Miss Madeley. Lord Trawden wishes me to inform you that he has business to tend to today and will join you later." The housekeeper walked over to where Antonia was standing. "He also asked me to give you this."

She handed Antonia a small ornate key and a note.

Where words fail, the violin reveals.

Looking down at the key, Antonia asked with confusion, "What does—"

"There is a surprise for you in the music gallery." She was about to ask where the room was when Bess clarified. "Across from the dining room, down the picture gallery."

Her heart began to soar. Clutching the key in her hand, she hurried from the room. "Thank you," she said over her shoulder. She wanted to prance down the hall, but settled on a brisk amble.

Bright sunlight filtered through the large gothic windows, carrying her toward her destination. By the time she reached the music gallery, she was giddy with excitement. Was it possible Dracon had a violin in residence for her to play?

When she entered the elegant gallery, peace and belonging washed over her. It was the room of her dreams. On one side, the length of the wall was lined with bookcases, and on the other, floor–to–ceiling windows overlooked a private courtyard. A pair of French doors opened out onto a lovely stone veranda that was shaded by a large oak tree. At opposite ends were matching white marble fireplaces, surrounded by an inviting arrangement of chairs and settees. A delicate pianoforte nearby beckoned to be played.

She was drawn to the piano, mesmerized by its beauty. As she neared, she noticed an oblong case on the bench.

Opening her hand, she stared down at the little key. Tears threatened to escape. The imprint of a ribbed crown interrupted the delicate lines running across her palm. She picked up the case and ran her hand across the intricate, heart-shaped scrollwork. Picking it up, she walked over to the crème settee, and sat, placing it on her lap.

The key fitted perfectly. A slight click interrupted the sound of her breathing. She lifted the smooth, richly varnished lid, and the familiar scent of spruce and maple soothed her to her soul. A pristine violin that looked as if it had never been played was nestled within the deep blue velvet-lined case. A jolt of excitement careened through her body, bringing back memories of her first instrument.

She lifted it from its cocoon and took her time inspecting the masterpiece, memorizing the smooth planes and intricate contours. After tuning the violin and preparing the bow, she retrieved her handkerchief, which was tucked in her sleeve, before lifting the violin by its neck. She placed the handkerchief above the bout, then nestled it under her chin.

It was as if this beautiful instrument had been made just for her.

The moment the bow caressed the strings, she was transported into another realm that existed only for her. Music that had been dormant in her mind for the past five years flowed through her hand. The world around her disappeared, except for the sweet sound of a melody.

♪♪♪

DRACON HAD STAYED AWAY LONGER than his business required. He had wanted to be present when Antonia opened the intricate wood case, but he was not prepared for the questions that would most likely follow, and thus, settled for being reclusive.

Strolling through the dark ground-level interior, he made his way to the grand staircase. The smooth legato of a violin drew him in, beckoning him just as a siren song called to a sailor. With each step, his surroundings lightened, and his soul became illuminated. The bay window on the first landing created an ethereal glow, embracing the angelic sound, guiding him toward his destiny.

Careful not to make his presence known, he glanced into the room. He spied Antonia, clearly lost in her music, near the pair of French doors. Her eyes were closed, her body moving in rhythm to her elegant strokes. It was the most beautiful sight he had beheld in years.

Standing outside the open gallery door, he leaned against the cool, white-paneled wall. Closing his eyes, he breathed in deeply, inhaling the melody as it filled his soul. From the first moment he had heard her play all those years ago, his soul had belonged to her.

How could he convince her that he was not the monster everyone believed him to be? How could he convince her that Catherine's death was an accident?

How could he convince her to give him another chance?

CHAPTER 7

The day before Christmas Eve had arrived, heralding her father's imminent return. Antonia's time at Lionshead would soon be at an end. Her heart lurched at the sobering thought. Remarkably, these last few days had brought such joy and happiness into her barren soul, and not just because of playing the violin, but also spending time with Dracon. He was strong yet soft, stern yet compassionate, and she was falling irrevocably in love with him.

She had been hoping to spend today with him, but her lady's maid informed her that he'd already left with his steward. She walked the length of her room several times. She was feeling better and in need of distraction. Of course, she could play her violin all day, but she needed to be useful, especially after all the attention and care she had received. Perhaps there was some task Bess could assign her. When she'd resided with Lady MacKinnon, her days had often been filled with sewing and needlework. Perhaps she should consider that as a parting gift, since she had nothing else to give.

With her mind made up, she left her room and went down

the hall to find Bess. As she rounded the corner, she bumped into Fulbert.

"Oh, pardon me, Miss Madeley," Fulbert apologized through composed features, despite the redness staining his face. He cleared his throat. "Miss Rede is here to see you. She is waiting in the downstairs drawing room."

Miss Rede knows I'm here?

Antonia forced a reply. "Thank you, Fulbert."

Trying to gather her senses, she made her way downstairs slowly. She was not prepared for seeing anyone. She stood outside the drawing room for an extra moment, squared her shoulders, took in a deep breath, and entered the room with a forced smile.

"Good morning, Miss Rede," she greeted as she entered the deep brown space. It was exactly as she remembered it, and in direct contrast to the rooms above. The heavy dark furniture and somber brown fabrics seemed to absorb all light and joy and tuck them away, never to be seen again.

Miss Rede rushed to her in a flurry of green Merino with extended arms, grasping both of her hands and squeezing none too gently. The gesture startled Antonia, sending a warning to her brain.

"I was so relieved to hear you survived that terrible accident," Miss Rede said in an overly sweet tone and with a wide, pasted on smile.

"You… how did you…"

"Dracon… oh, I mean Lord Trawden, informed me. We are often in each other's company."

Antonia was irked by Miss Rede's casual use of Dracon's name.

"How. Are. You?" Miss Rede annunciated each word with artificial concern.

Antonia pulled her hands from the other woman's clawlike grasp and wiped them down the front of her dress. "I am quite recov—" Her reply was interrupted by Miss Rede's observation.

"I must say, I was surprised to hear that you are convalescing at Lionshead, what with your father's estate being so near." She eyed Antonia with hawk-like eyes, almost as if surveying her prey.

"The weather—" For the second time in a short span Miss Rede interrupted Antonia. The woman was quickly outstaying her welcome.

"Yes, I suppose that would have been a factor." Miss Rede walked over to one of the large tapestries. Inspecting it with fervor, she spoke over her shoulder, "It is nice for Lord Trawden to have company. This is a difficult time of year for him. When I saw him last, he was not quite himself. I suppose the loss of my cousin still grieves him greatly. They were so much in love."

The mention of Dracon's late wife cast a dark shadow on Antonia's heart. As she feared, the memory of Catherine would always be present. But there was a greater question she must contemplate…

Bringing a hand to her temple, she claimed fatigue. "I apologize, but I am not feeling quite up to par yet."

"Oh, it's quite all right. I do wish you well, Miss Madeley." Miss Rede's tone was laced with a faux sweetness that capped Antonia's sour mood.

Without further acknowledgment, Antonia left the room. The visit had left her all out of sorts. She felt as if a cold hand from the grave had reached out and closed around her heart and squeezed some of her newfound joy.

Was Miss Rede being truthful? Antonia had always suspected that Dracon *was* still mourning Catherine's death. But over the past days, something had shifted between herself and him. Could there still be hope for them? Through the haze of a multitude of confusing thoughts and emotions, a small voice of reason whispered in her head not to believe everything Miss Rede had said.

After that unpleasant encounter, she was determined to bring some semblance of joy to the day and decided to seek out Bess and inquire after some useful task.

The common area below stairs was quite large and nicely appointed, with a long table and numerous chairs. Despite the cool day outside, the room was warm and filled with the scent of spiced apples that drifted from down the hall. Bess and several other women were busy sewing and did not see Antonia enter.

"What are you working on?" she said in a cheerful voice.

Several pairs of startled eyes flashed up, settling on Antonia.

Bess' gaze darted between the other servants before she answered with some hesitation. "It is tradition for those at Lionshead to make quilts and handkerchiefs and such things for the less fortunate in the village and distribute them during Christmastide. These are the last of the items to be completed and are for the Widow Wilson. Her husband died a few months ago leaving her with two wee ones."

Antonia's heart jolted with the thought of the young widow enduring a Christmas without her beloved, and wanted to lend a hand. "That is most charitable. Would you mind if I assisted?"

Bess stilled with an odd stare, as if Antonia's request was so out of the ordinary it was not to be believed. Another moment passed before Bess responded, "Yes, I suppose it's acceptable. That would be most helpful." She gathered a basket of unfinished items and handed it to Antonia. "Perhaps you would be more comfortable in the drawing room."

Antonia did not want to seem like an intruder, but desired company more than anything else at the moment. "I am quite at ease below stairs. My position…" She was not ashamed of her position as Lady MacKinnon's companion, only her actions leading up to her employment. Her voice sounded meek, even to her own ears. "If you don't mind, I would enjoy working here."

Bess offered kind reassurance. "Not at all, Miss Madeley."

Antonia smiled, then began working on finishing the edges of a small blanket. "Did Lady Trawden start this tradition?" The words exited her mouth before she could stop them.

"No," one of the other servants firmly replied.

Heat rushed up her cheeks. "I'm sorry, I shouldn't have…"

"Oh, no, Miss Madeley, it isn't that, it's just…" Bess paused, almost as if she were revealing something she shouldn't. "Lord Trawden's wife… tended to other duties. His mother, on the other hand, was most generous." As if realizing she had said too much, Bess clamped her mouth shut.

That was a peculiar comment. Antonia always assumed that Dracon's first wife was the epitome of a proper marchioness—confidant, always doing and saying the right things, and never, ever, mis-stepping.

Sensing a quiet tension passing between those assembled, Antonia began to chatter nervously about anything that came to mind. "Lady MacKinnon insisted we make things for the less fortunate, not just during Christmastide, but all year. It was a pleasant way to pass the time. However, my favorite part was delivering the items."

"Indeed, it is a joy to help those in need," one of the parlor maids said.

With the first blanket completed, Antonia turned her attention to another one in her pile. She stared down at the soft fabric in hand. A sadness washed over her once more at the thought of those little children being without their father for Christmastide. "I was just thinking, what if we assemble baskets with various foodstuffs to go along with these items?"

"That is a wonderful idea," Bess exclaimed with delight. "I will have Fulbert gather baskets. Oh, and I'm sure Cook has already prepared her Christmastide treats."

The mood of the room brightened. Suddenly Antonia no longer felt like an intruder, but a welcomed participant. After her initial suggestion, everyone gave their input, and for the next couple of hours, Bess and Antonia collected and arranged all the items that were to be included in the baskets.

"What's this all about?" Dracon's deep voice disrupted the merriment in progress.

"We are assembling baskets to be distributed to those less fortunate," Antonia muttered uneasily. Would he think her too presumptuous to have suggested this without his approval?

Dracon stepped closer, eyeing the assembly. "Was this your idea?" He looked at her, not in anger, but in surprise.

"Well, Bess and Cook and—"

"Miss Madeley is too modest by far, my lord. When she heard that Widow Wilson was struggling this season, she insisted on making up baskets for her and her wee ones, and for the other families, as well."

Antonia turned to him, her face hot with embarrassment. She swallowed hard. "I hope you don't mind. I just thought it would be a nice Christmas surprise."

"On the contrary, I believe it is a marvelous idea." His smile widened in approval.

"Would you like to help?" The words poured from her without consideration. But she was sincere in her offer and hoped he would accept.

Dracon seemed as shy and unsure as she felt. "I...I would enjoy that very much. Lead the way."

She offered him a warm smile. "Let's get to work, then." She took charge of organizing the basket assembly, and much to her surprise, Dracon did not seem to mind.

On occasion, she would glance over to where he was diligently tying bows to the basket handles. As if feeling her gaze, he'd raise his head, and the heat of his stare would distract her, sending her thoughts in an entirely inappropriate direction. Or was she reading too much into his smoldering regard that warmed... *Oh dear*, but her insides were all knotted in an all too pleasant way.

Several hours later, she stood on the threshold of Lionshead, wrapped in a cloak, attempting to ward off the chill of the day, and watching as dozens of decorated baskets were being loaded onto the wagon. She was proud of their accomplishment. But more than anything, she felt as if a dormant part of her had come back to life. She missed being part of a family.

Dracon turned away from the wagon. His intense gaze met hers, sending a warm, tingling shiver down to her toes.

"You're cold." Dracon's words were laced with concern. "I think it best that you stay inside. I will see that these are delivered safely."

He bowed, then took his leave toward the stables, leaving Antonia to contemplate the past, the torrent of feelings rushing through her, and what she wanted for the future.

♪♪♪

THE WEATHER HAD TURNED MISERABLE, but thankfully all the baskets had been delivered. Dracon couldn't wait to tell Antonia how grateful everyone had been. He had sent Elmer back with the cart while he continued on horseback. During the course of the afternoon, he realized that, with each passing hour, he was falling more in love with Antonia. Her kind heart and generosity only intensified his simmering desire for her.

The time had come to put his house in order, to let go of the past, and embrace the future. But first, he had to reconcile with the ghosts of his former life to have a future with Antonia. He had wasted too many years brooding over events he could not change. He would be damned if he let them dictate his life anymore.

He rode through the thick, hazy fog that seemed to be swallowing the landscape. He could not even see ten feet in front of him. His senses were on high alert, listening for anyone who might dare to venture out on such a miserable day. Christmas Eve was tomorrow and, regardless of weather, there was something he had to do.

The square, grey-stoned tower rose above the fog, guiding Dracon toward his destination. The old archway that led into the churchyard came into view, followed by dozens of gravestones marking the passing of those old and young, but his destination was not outside.

Dismounting Thuban, he tied the horse to an obliging tree and walked toward the west entrance. It had been over nine years since he had ventured here. He pushed on the heavy wood door and it opened with a loud creak. A blast of cool air whipped across his face, and the stale smell of burnt candles tickled his nostrils. He walked into the frigid space, hardly noticing the statues honoring the deceased. The clerestory windows allowed the miserable day to infiltrate the sacred space. At the south end, tucked away in a recessed nook, a white marble angel cried over a woman and a baby that lay lifeless in his celestial arms.

Catherine and their unborn babe.

Tears stung the corners of his eyes as he ran his hand over the inscription. When Catherine and their child died, he had retreated from all society, suffering alone in silence. He went to London only to see his sister and to tend to his duties, but preferred spending time in the country, far away from the gossiping mouths and prying eyes of the *ton*. He had cloistered himself away from any possible joy.

Five years ago, he had thought he was ready to marry again and would have done everything in his power to make Antonia happy, but he had been unwilling to completely let go of the past. He had closed off his heart and his soul, not letting anyone in for fear of losing again. Not even Antonia, even although she'd touched him deeply in a way no other had. He realized that now and prayed it was not too late.

Only recently, had he come to terms with Catherine's death. He knew it had not been his fault that she had tripped and fallen down the stairs, but he had continued to blame himself until, once again, he heard Antonia play the violin.

In the span of a couple of measures, she had recaptured his heart. He had been mesmerized by the short and long strokes, the movement of her hand guiding her bow across her violin's strings. The music she conjured from the eloquent instrument had amazed him, but even more mesmerizing was the way she played. The passion she exhibited had awoken a part of him that he was certain had been asleep since the day he was born. His world was no longer black and white, but filled with vivid shades in every color imaginable. He did not want to return to his former way of life.

He was tired of living in the shadow of death. Bending his

head down, he pressed his forehead against the weeping angel's. "I'm sorry I failed you, Catherine. Please forgive me." His hoarse whisper echoed through the still air.

His head snapped up as sounds of the door opening and closing collided with his apology. A blast of frigid wind swirled through the nave. He glanced about, but saw no one. Unexpected sunlight filtered in through the stained glass in the windows, sending brilliant hues of blue, yellow, and red dancing across the floor.

A sense of peace washed over him. At long last, he was able to let go of the past.

CHAPTER 8

*I*f it wasn't unlucky to put up decorations before Christmas Eve, Dracon would have done it sooner. Antonia had brought such happiness into his life, he wanted to share it with everyone. And there was no better time of year to spread such joy.

Holly, rosemary, and evergreens had been gathered to adorn the house. Ribbons of gold intertwined with long garlands of ivy, boughs of holly embellished with silver tinsel, and ornamented wreaths were all ready to be hung. All that was missing was Antonia, but he suspected he'd have to wait a little longer before she emerged from her violin practice.

He did not know what Christmas traditions she celebrated, but when he was a young boy, his whole family had gathered and decorated together. The music gallery was one of his favorite rooms. His mother had always insisted the Yule log be lit in one of the two fireplaces on opposite sides of the room, instead of in the drawing room. Sadly, with his mother's death, that tradition had died as well. But now he wanted to rekindle the tradition and share it with someone else—someone he loved.

He had already hung several boughs of mistletoe and was busy organizing the numerous piles of greenery when Antonia entered the gallery.

"Good evening," she said with a vibrancy that warmed his heart. "I thought you said you never get into mischief." She waved her hand. "Look at this mess," she pretended to admonish with a bright smile.

He felt more like a schoolboy than a grown man. He teased in return, "Would you care to help me clean it up?" She raised a quizzical brow, then he added, "Actually, I thought we might decorate together."

She clasped her hands in excitement and eyed him with a playful glint. "I would love to. It has been such a long time and…"

Not for the first time, he wondered what had happened in her life to cause such restraint. He would not push his advantage, but at some time in the near future, he fully intended on discovering all of her secrets.

Except for Antonia humming Christmas carols, they decorated together in quiet companionship. He was enjoying watching her as she put her heart into each creation. She picked up a piece of evergreen and attached several little apples and an elegant red bow. Within a matter of moments, she had created an elegant display and begun on the next.

"Is there any white ribbon?" she asked as she assembled another swag. "I think the contrast is ever so lovely between the white ribbon and the green."

He would have given her miles of white ribbon just to hear the joy in her voice.

"They're here, Lord Trawden," Bess' squeal of delight rang from down the hall.

Antonia glanced at him with confused interest, but did not say a word. He strolled to her side and offered his arm. "Shall we?"

DRACON GUIDED Antonia down the grand staircase, past the bay of five stained-glass windows on the first landing. Dozens of candles had been lit. The alcove glowed in soft shades of red and green. Antonia thought it was a magical, mystical sight.

"What is…?"

Her words faded as they took the last flight of stairs. Below them in the entry hall stood three farmworkers with the largest log she had ever seen in her life.

Dracon praised the men. "Excellent job. It is the largest Yule log yet." Pride shone on the men's faces at Dracon's praise. He then turned to Antonia. "In which fireplace would you like the Yule log to be placed?"

He was *asking* her?

The fact that he sought to include her in making a decision about his household sparked her to hope for more. Her cheeks warmed and butterflies fluttered through her stomach. "Would the music gallery be suitable? It is my favorite room."

Her response earned her a wide smile that crescendoed the butterflies into stampeding intensity. "That was my choice as well."

The Yule log was delivered to the gallery and, before long, was lit, providing added warmth. They resumed decorating, sharing family traditions and happy memories.

"When I was little and my father was away, Mother and I would often sit by the fire. She would read and I would play the violin."

"It sounds like heaven."

"It was." Antonia's heart softened with thoughts of her mother. "Those evenings by the fire with my mother were some of the happiest of my childhood." She met his gaze. "I shall play for you later this evening if you would like."

"I would be honored." His words touched her heart and warmed her insides.

This is how she had always imagined life would be—peaceful evenings, filled with conversation and music.

An hour in domestic bliss had passed. She had never enjoyed being with anyone as much as she enjoyed being with Dracon. She attached a piece of holly and a delicate white ribbon on the base of a candelabrum. Satisfied with her creation, she backed up toward the door, surveying their work.

"I think it is quite lovely." Truthfully, it was the loveliest room she had ever seen. It looked like a place where magical things could happen.

"Why did you run off?" His question, bold and direct, came from out of nowhere, catching her off guard.

All the joy she had felt a moment ago faded. She stood silent, unsure how to even answer the question. It was the moment she had been dreading.

Dracon ran a hand through his glorious dark hair. A look of pain—or perhaps regret—flashed in his blue eyes before he regained his usual composure. "I would have released you from our engagement if you had just talked to me." He held her gaze with an honest sincerity that almost frightened her.

She turned away, unable to bear his scrutiny. Leaning against the doorjamb, she answered over her shoulder. "We would never have suited."

He walked up behind her, his strength surrounding her.

"How would you know?" His deep voice sent a tingling down her spine. "You never even let me kiss you."

She turned around, surprised and uncertain, and more curious than ever. He lifted his hand slowly, as if unsure of how she would react. His warm palm cupped her cheek, his thumb caressing in such a way that made her whole body come to life.

"We're standing under the mistletoe." She felt his words rush through her moments before his lips came down on hers.

His kiss was soft and gentle, nothing like she had imagined it would be. She melted into his arms, letting him support her, carrying her away on a billowy cloud of hope. She tried to control all the delicious feelings he stirred within. She tried to tell herself it would only lead to heartache. She tried to convince herself it was all a façade and that he could not possibly care for her. But she had desired him for far too long.

He pulled back, ever so slightly. His seductive words whispered across her lips, "I believe we would have suited just fine."

She did not know what was going to happen next, but she knew what she wanted to happen. Unfortunately, Dracon's decision differed from hers.

"Before I do something improper, I must bid you goodnight." He brushed a kiss over her cheek. "Until tomorrow, my Antonia."

CHAPTER 9

❧

*I*t was Christmas Day, the house looked beautiful with all the decorations in place, and… Antonia was baffled and all out of sorts. The kiss she'd shared with Dracon was nothing like anything she'd ever experienced, but his abrupt departure had left her confused. Worse, she had yet to see him today. Was he avoiding her? Did he regret kissing her?

And then there was her father, who still had not returned from Bath, at least, if he had, she hadn't been made aware. Her aunt's dire letter had made it sound as if he was on his deathbed, but from what Antonia had discerned from Dracon, Father was still quite hale.

She shook out her hands, trying to ease the building tension. She needed to release all the anxiety coursing through her. She needed…. to play the violin.

The afternoon sunlight filtered in through the hall windows, taunting her still-sensitive head. Shielding her eyes, she quickened her pace. The fresh scent of evergreens carried her down the bright hall. For the first time in a week, she felt more like herself than she had in ages.

When she entered the bright music gallery, the spicy scents of rosemary and mistletoe tickled her senses, reminding her of the kiss she'd shared with Dracon last evening. Her cheeks warmed, and her lips burned in remembrance. She wanted to experience more… with him, and only him.

She glanced about the festive space. Everything looked even more exquisite in the daylight. The mantel, however, was her favorite. Decorated with an elaborate evergreen swag strewn with silver ribbons, it was the stuff of which her Christmastide dreams were made. In the span of twenty-four hours, not only had the gallery been transformed into a winter paradise, but she had somehow transformed as well.

Even though five years ago she'd tried to convince herself that she had not wanted to marry Dracon, her heart betrayed her. During these past years, she had thought of him more times than she could count. She had often wondered what life would have been like with him instead of the lonely existence she had created for herself. But she had been young, naïve, and foolish back then, and since, the world had taught her many lessons. Even Dracon's stoic mannerisms no longer frightened her, quite the opposite, in fact. She found him intriguing and full of depth and desire. The key he had given her not only unlocked a cherished instrument, but in many ways, he had discovered the key to her heart.

She strode to the table and picked up the elegant violin, then retreated to her room. Since Dracon was busy visiting several of the tenant farmers, and Christmas dinner would not be served for a couple more hours, there was plenty of time to compose a special sonata for him. He had given her so much, and she wanted to share her love of music with him.

The quartet of putti smiling down on her provided the perfect inspiration. She brought the violin up to her cheek, the sweet, rich smell of wood soothing her soul. She would never tire of its scent. Bringing the lower bout to her neck, she raised the bow to the bridge and applied light pressure while gliding it over the strings. A smooth, continuous tone drifted through the air. Her hands took control, dictating the rhythm, and she lost herself in the melody she was making for the man she had fallen in love with.

♪♪♪

DRACON STROLLED DOWN the bright corridor, drawn by the melodious sound emanating from the white suite. He halted in the open doorway, resting against the jamb. Antonia's back was toward him, and she was playing with such passion, such intensity, that he wanted to be part of it.

The sway of her lithe, petite form mesmerized him as she played. One elegant hand held the bow as it glided across the strings, hypnotizing him with a slow, seductive sound. Her long, wavy brown hair cascaded across her back like waves upon the shore, undulating to the notes she evoked from her instrument.

She turned around, and their eyes met in a seductive dance. Slowly, she walked toward him, never stopping playing. "You're watching me," she whispered with a smile.

"I could watch you play for all eternity."

She stood a couple of feet from him. Soon, the melody softened and slowed to a gentle end. She lowered the bow to her side.

Heat swirled around them. She stared at him with a questioning desire that he wanted to answer.

"Please don't stop." His heart hammered against his chest.

She worried her lip for a moment before shyly replying, "I wanted it to be a surprise for you."

He crossed the threshold, but still unsure, kept his distance. "It is magnificent. You play beautifully, my Antonia." He wanted her to play more, just for him. "I enjoy your music."

Something powerful passed between them. He could feel it like a current in the air.

"Do you play?" she questioned.

"No." He was embarrassed by his answer.

"Whyever not?" Her brows crinkled together in a most delectable way.

Dracon looked down at his large, awkward hands. He could never create such an exquisite sound. She shifted her bow into her other hand, and then took his hand. The warmth from her ungloved skin ricocheted through his veins.

"Come, let me show you."

He closed the door to the outside world, not wanting anyone besides Antonia to witness the failure that was certain to follow. He went with her to the center of the room. The putti above mocked him with their laughter.

"Take the violin into your left hand."

"This isn't going to…"

She stepped back and looked into his eyes, daring him to challenge her. "Stop being difficult and at least try."

Placing the violin into position, he awaited the next set of orders. It was taking all his willpower to focus on the instrument and not kiss her. Without words, she placed the bow into his right hand, then adjusted his fingers into the correct position and stood behind his right arm. He glanced down at her, the top of her head barely reaching his shoulder.

Her hand smoothed over his, and she began to guide the bow across the strings. A high-pitched squeal sent a sharp shiver down his spine. He began to back away when Antonia's petite frame halted him.

"Even the most experienced violinists can match that sound. Your left wrist needs to be firm." Dracon obliged and earned her praise in return. "Good. Now, just relax."

Easier said than done when she was standing so close, her spicy scent muddling his thoughts, sending his senses in a spiral of desire. He sucked in his breath, trying to focus on the lesson.

Just as she had done before, she guided his right hand and bow across the strings. This time, however, the soft, sweet sound was music to his ears. She leaned in closer, continuing to guide him, his elbow nestling against her soft flesh.

He looked down into her dancing green eyes. "Antonia," he whispered. The music halted and was replaced with an entirely different sort of rhythm.

She came around to face him. With the bow still resting against the strings, her hand traveled up the length of his arm. His breathing increased, and he wanted nothing more than to pull her into his embrace and kiss her, but something held him back. This was her moment to explore and determine the next course of action. No matter how much he wanted her, Dracon wanted her to decide.

Antonia took the bow and violin from his hand, then placed it gingerly on an obliging side table. She moved closer to him with passion in her eyes. Within seconds she was at his side and resuming her exploration, her hands roaming over the width of his chest.

"Your heartbeat is *prestissimo*. Very fast." Her hands ran up his neck. Did she have any idea how attractive she was to him? "Kiss me," she ordered in a seductive tone. "Please."

He leaned in and took her mouth in a soft exploratory action, drinking in the sweetness of her lips. But it wasn't enough. His lips continued to discover her soft ivory flesh, trailing kisses down her neck.

"Dracon." His name on her breath was a delicious aphrodisiac.

Scooping her up, he carried her to the large chair beside the fireplace. He sat down with her in his arms, never breaking their kiss. He wanted to show her all the love he felt for her, but there were still so many unanswered questions. He did not want to begin the next chapter of their lives with ghosts of the past lingering between them.

"We cannot do this," he said between kisses, trying his best to be a gentleman but failing miserably.

"Oh." She tried to push herself off his lap, but he kept her firmly in place.

Dracon had never been a conversationalist. He had always been the one to give orders, take care of business, hide his feelings. But with Antonia, it was different. He wanted to hold her in his arms and talk for hours, kiss her for days, love her for an eternity.

He gently caressed her face. "I don't want you to leave." He looked deep into her eyes and saw desire mixed with apprehension. How could he explain that not only did he desire her in his bed but in his life, as his wife? Part of him was afraid that she would run away again and that he would lose her forever.

She edged down and rested her head on his chest, seemingly lost in her thoughts. Her long fingers swirled patterns across his chest before coming to rest right above his pounding heart, which had been locked away for far too long.

The silence persisted, but Dracon could sense she was working through past events, just as he had done. Words wrestled in his mind as he held her. In the end, he settled for simplicity.

"Antonia, talk to me."

♪♪♪

"TALK TO ME." Those three simple words held a world of anxiety for Antonia.

"I can't. You'll be angry." She gulped down on the hard lump in her throat. Over the past week, the love she'd always felt for him had deepened into something more. She didn't just love him, she had fallen *in love* with him. He was thoughtful, kind, and generous. And nothing like her father. She might not be the love of his life, but she knew they could be happy together. She feared her answers would cause their fragile beginning to crumble.

"I'm not going to be angry with you. Just tell me what happened. Tell me why you left."

Something deep inside urged her to confess. If they were to have a future together, she must. She closed her eyes tight and held her breath as she blurted the words forth. "I didn't elope. It was all a lie. I made it all up. I traveled up to Gretna Green with my lady's maid, who was dressed as a gentleman. I sent word to my father that I had married."

"You never married?" Confusion laced each syllable.

"No."

His words came out on a relieved sigh. "You're not married." He raised her chin, forcing her to look at him. He did not say another word, but continued to gaze into her tear-filled eyes. Moments passed before he whispered, "My Antonia, what caused you to run away?" He brushed a soft and gentle kiss to her lips.

The heat from her cheeks rushed to her head, and her breath quickened with restrained emotion. Shaking her head, she wanted to tell him everything but... "I can't. It's just too—"

"Please... I just want to know."

Pain coursed through her heart. She had wasted so much time. She took in a deep breath to garner some courage, then released it rapidly. Once she began, the words flowed in a continuous stream. "My lady's maid helped me before returning home to her mother. I sold my violin, pretended to be a widow, and forged several letters of recommendation to gain employment as a companion to Lady MacKinnon. I've been pretending to be someone I wasn't for the past five years."

There, it was done. Her humiliation was complete.

"Why didn't you just return home?"

She worried her bottom lip, trying to garner the courage. "I was embarrassed and humiliated and... I couldn't face you, not after what I did."

He lifted her chin with a gentle finger. "You never have to fear me."

"I don't fear you."

Quite the contrary.

How was she to tell him she never had feared him, that she had loved him from the very first moment? But despite her feelings, she knew in her heart she would always come second to the memory of his beloved first wife. Theirs had been a romantic love match with which she could never compete. No, some things were better left unsaid.

His brows drew together with confusion. "Then why did you run away?"

She took in another deep breath, and then on a long slow exhale, started to explain, "When my mother was dying, she said things about my father and..." The words stuck in her throat.

Kissing the top of her head, he said, "If it is too painful to…"

She lifted her head to meet his gaze. "No, it's not, it's just…. I wasted so much time trying not to be like her." She sniffled back the sobs. "Don't you understand? I don't want to be like her." The hot tears cascaded down her cheeks. "I…"

She shook her head and tried to turn away, but Dracon cupped her face, demanding her attention. "You are talented and beautiful and have so much life."

"Really?" She sniffled back the tears.

"Yes." He held her firmly to him, caressing her back. "What did your mother say?"

Antonia had never revealed that final conversation with anyone. It had been too much of a shock. "She… she said I was just like her, and that I would make the same mistake and be trapped in misery."

"Trapped?" His voice cracked with restrained emotion.

She couldn't tell him the whole truth. He'd hate her forever, and she couldn't—no, wouldn't—lose this second opportunity to be happy. It had taken five long years and a carriage accident to learn that she could accept that Dracon could never love her with the same intensity as his first wife. But he deserved to know at least part of the truth.

"Mother said that she gave up everything she loved when she married Father. She had enjoyed music and dancing, and even played the violin, but Father detests the instrument. I was only allowed to play because he was away so frequently." Her voice drifted into a hushed whisper. "Her words scared me."

Gently, he stroked her cheek. "You do not have to give up

anything to be with me. That is not what I want." His gaze softened. "Don't you know that?"

In that moment she realized he was not what she thought him to be. He was so much more. "I know that now." She gazed into his eyes and for the first time, really saw *him*. He was caring and forgiving, dedicated and loyal, and stoic yet soft. She'd often dreamed of being within his embrace, and now that she was here, she didn't quite know what to do. "Dracon…"

He lowered his head and took her mouth in a sensuous kiss. His tender lips explored and coaxed. Her arms encircled his neck, pulling him even closer, wanting to feel his sheer strength pressed hard against her body. She roamed one hand down his arm, relishing in the feel of his firm muscles. Lost in the sensations he stirred, she returned his kiss with a fiery intensity that seemed to surprise them both.

He pulled back, breathing heavily. "Antonia, I am trying to be a gentleman and…"

She touched one finger to his lips, silencing him as she shook her head. "I don't want you to be a gentleman." She smiled, hoping to hide some of the nervous anticipation she was feeling. "I just want you."

His blue eyes deepened, filling with desire. She reached up and kissed his lips with all the love she felt in her heart, her soul, for him, and only him.

Her heart danced with excitement when he stood, keeping her within the folds of his arms. As he moved toward the bed, their clothes came off with all the urgency that had been in her kiss a few moments before, and then they stood before each other, completely naked. There was no shyness, just simmering desire to touch and discover.

He inhaled deeply as if trying to control the rising desire, but didn't move or say a word, as he let her explore. She let her hands roam across his wide, muscular chest as if she were playing a new song. The cords of muscle were smooth and taut. She brushed soft kisses across his chest. His scent was an intoxicating combination of spice and countryside that made her want to do things she didn't even know the names for.

Gently, he eased her down on the bed. "I want you, my Antonia," he whispered before reclaiming her lips in a soul-searching kiss.

And she knew in that moment that her heart would never be the same.

DRACON HAD WAITED five years for this. There was no other woman in the world he wanted to share his life with. He had not been able to express his feelings to her all those years ago —sentimental words had never come easily to him, but he fully intended on showing her how much he cared for her.

As his lips reveled in her delectable softness, she arched her back, inviting him to take all she had to offer. He brushed feather-light kisses down her silky chest before taking one hardened bud in his mouth. He drank in the sweetness of her body, nibbling until he heard her cry out in pleasure. With each sigh and moan, his desire rose. He ran his tongue down one beautiful breast, across the delicate spot on her chest, then kissed his way to the other nipple. He wanted to savor her body with every lick, every kiss, and every nibble. She was the music that fed his soul.

He weaved a trail of feathered kisses down her stomach, relishing in the feel of her creamy skin. His hands delighted in the curves of her body, gliding lower until he reached her warm curls.

A loud gasp followed by a soft sigh of pleasure escaped

her lips as he teased the opening of her feminine core with his finger, then pushed forward. He kissed his way back up to her lips, wanting to feel her moans of pleasure. Her kiss sang through his veins. The feel of her hands exploring his back was divine ecstasy. He wanted more, needed more, more of her. He shifted position, pressing himself against her. Her soft curves molded to his body. They were made for each other.

"*My* Antonia," he muttered before easing into her. In that moment there were no secrets between them; nothing but the joining of two souls meant to be together.

Their eyes locked. Antonia had captured his heart five years ago, and now she captured his soul for all eternity.

"You are mine," he whispered. He broke through her barrier, claiming her.

"Always," she cried out in sweet agony as he filled her.

He stilled, waiting for her to adjust to his invasion. The world around them faded. He had waited his whole life for this moment. There was no other way to describe it: Antonia made him feel alive.

Moans of pleasure filled the room. He felt her start to lose control as her body quivered, finding release. Her cry of delight inflamed his desire, and within moments, his own body shuddered, sending waves of pleasure crashing through him. *Antonia was his*.

Burying his face in her neck, he caressed her glistening skin with kisses. Gathering her into his arms, he rolled onto his back, smoothing damp, long locks of golden-brown hair from her face as he brought the blanket around them. Antonia's body relaxed against his, and her breathing evened. Their rapid heartbeats slowed in unison.

She sighed against his chest and murmured, "I love you," before she drifted off to sleep.

He kissed the top of her head. *I love you, my Antonia*.

CHAPTER 10

*a*ntonia had spent a glorious night in Dracon's arms. She had revealed *some* of her fears. However, there were things she would never reveal. He cared for her and she knew in her heart they could find happiness together, and that was all that mattered. She rolled onto her back, stretching her aching limbs. This was an ache she could get used to enjoying.

With her morning ablutions completed, she dressed and, with giddy excitement, headed for the breakfast room. She could not wait to see him. In the wee hours of the night, they had made plans for the day after Christmas, and passing out presents to the staff. It was another time-honored tradition that had died with her mother.

Antonia had just reached the day parlor when a familiar voice echoing around the Grand Hall halted her steps.

"I will ask only one more time. Where is she?" The loud voice demanded, ricocheting through the dark downstairs passages.

Father.

She rushed down the stairs, her hand gliding across the

rail. She looked down at the two men. Dracon stood with his arms crossed, the stoic mask she detested firmly in place. Their eyes met. She saw all the pain and loss that still resided in his heart. Biting her lip, she looked away.

She *knew* he was thinking about his late wife who had died on these stairs. A tremor of anguish shot through her. All the joy she had been experiencing shattered into a thousand pieces. Her heart withered inside. What had she done?

By the time she reached the last steps, her pace had slowed to a trudge. Her father's countenance had changed from belligerence to tolerance. With a wide smile plastered to his face, he opened his arms, and she walked straight into them. In the blink of an eye, her world had changed, and not for the better.

"Oh, my dear, how I've missed you." Although his words sounded sincere, there was an underlying meaning that she could not quite place.

"I missed you too, Father." The words were not a lie, but the meaning was somehow lost. Her initial reason for coming had been replaced with something more precious and delicate. She was barely able to contain her emotions and could not even attempt to look at Dracon.

"We are returning home *immediately*. I don't want to spend another moment without you."

Antonia did not think it possible, but the fragile pieces of her heart shattered even more.

She wanted Dracon to fight for her, but he just stood there mute. He had told her last night he wanted her to spend time with her father—to find peace with her sire, but she did not think Dracon would send her away, not after all they had shared. She thought he wanted her—wanted her to be his wife. Clearly, she was wrong. What had happened to change his mind?

Her father spoke as if Dracon was not present. "I informed Lord Trawden you would be residing at Madeley Hall and that no further contact would be necessary. We best be on our way. Your stepmother is anxious to see you."

Antonia was about to protest when Dracon spoke up. "I would like a brief word with Antonia."

Her father glared at Dracon, but relented when she squeezed his arm. "I will be waiting outside. Don't be long, daughter."

She did not know why her father had such disdain for Dracon, but was thankful for the few minutes alone with him.

Once her father was out of earshot, Dracon approached, his manner calm and in control. "I think it best that you spend Christmastide with him. He is quite pleased that he will have you home." He leaned in and brushed a single kiss across her cheek. "I will forward your things."

And just like that, she was brushed aside.

Surely something had transpired between her father and Dracon. Why else would he be acting in such a manner? She wanted answers. "Why are you sending me away?"

"It's Christmas. You should be with your family." Dracon's reasoning made sense, but that didn't explain his sudden change in behavior.

She could not hide the hurt from her voice. "What about last night?"

He ran a trembling hand through his dark hair. "Antonia, please—"

"No. I want to know."

Dracon's voice was monotone and distant. "We will discuss it later. Your *father* is waiting." A shadow swept across his face before he turned and walked away.

With slow, heavy steps, she walked outside into the bitter cold and entered the waiting carriage. What had just happened? She could not believe that their time together was at an end. This *had* to be her father's doing. There was no other explanation for the way Dracon dismissed her after all they had shared over the past week.

She had barely sat down in the conveyance when the accusation flew from her mouth. "What did you say to him?"

"Only that I wanted to spend time with my daughter." Her father's carefree, nonchalant tone was a reminder of how he dealt with things. Whenever he did not want to discuss something, his tone turned light, and dismissive.

"But—" She had not even managed to utter another word when her father began to set out all his plans.

"We will hold a spectacular soirée in celebration of your return and your upcoming—"

"Why do you not care for Lord Trawden?"

There was a long silence. She could see that he was trying to formulate some excuse, and when it came, it was indifferent and without true emotion. "He was the reason you left."

"Drac… Lord Trawden was not the only reason why I left." Dracon wasn't even the main reason why she'd run away. No, her mother's confession, and Father's lack of propriety and not caring for her feelings had shattered her. "I wanted—"

"Dearest, there will be time enough to relive the past. Right now, I just want to enjoy your company before we reach home."

Antonia was loath to ask, but felt obligated just the same. "How does your wife fair?"

"Lady Madeley is quite well. Perhaps you have not heard, my wife is *enceinte* again," he said with pride-tinged arrogance. "I am hoping for another son."

"I suppose felicitations are in order." She could not hide

the sarcasm from her voice. She had always known her father had been disappointed *she* was not a son.

After her mother died, Antonia had assumed at some point her father would marry again. His greatest wish had gone unfulfilled, and she did not think he would rest until he had an heir. But marrying Antonia's friend by special license the day after his official mourning period was over had been too much to bear.

Father eyed her with disdain from the corner of his eye. "I do wish you would not take that tone. I have waited a long time to have such blessings."

"At my expense and Mother's," Antonia said with a harshness that took them both aback.

"I suggest you rein in your temper before we arrive. I will not tolerate such behavior." Her father's words held a warning that sent a shiver down her spine. She would have to tread lightly.

When she had received her aunt's note that Father was ill, all she could think about was being with him. But now that she was sitting beside him, all she wanted to do was leave his presence and be with Dracon.

Heat rose in her cheeks as remembrances of the beautiful evening she had shared with Dracon came back to her in vivid recollection. The feel of his large hands stroking the length of her body, the way his mouth…

"Are you still ill?"

Her father's question broke the spell she was under.

"No, I am quite recovered, as it would appear you are." She could not help the sour retort. *So much for treading lightly.*

"What is that supposed to mean?"

It was time for him to answer some of her questions. "Aunt Rowena said in her letter that you were ill."

Father's mouth curved into a slight frown. "I suppose I was for a brief time, but I went to Bath and now I am quite recovered." Appearing insensitive to her concerns, Father changed the course of conversation and chattered about his new life. "Yuletide festivities will be commencing this evening. My wife's family descended on us yesterday and will be in attendance for the duration. When we arrive at Madeley Hall, I expect you to display the utmost respect to your mother."

Anger crescendoed with each word she spoke. "She is *not* my mother." Hester had betrayed Antonia's trust and seduced her father while he was in mourning. "*My* mother is no longer of this earth. Miss Uppington was one of my dearest friends until—"

"I will not discuss this yet again. Your mother is dead," he stated matter-of-factly, as if talking about the state of the roads or the weather. "Hester is my wife now, and I fully expect you to accept her." He turned his gaze toward the passing landscape. Without bothering to look at her, he said, "I don't want to dwell on the past. It darkens my mood."

Nothing had changed. That Antonia expected it would was folly. She felt as if she were an orphan. Her mother was gone, and her father was indifferent toward her. If it were not for Aunt Rowena, she would be truly alone in the world.

They sat with no more words between them as the carriage lumbered along, the only sound coming from the wheels struggling through the mud. Antonia's nerves became jumpy as memories of the accident overtook her mind. She clutched the side of the seat, desperate to find stability. Her breath came in short spurts, and she fought to remain calm. Images of those final moments flashed before her—Mallory's insulting words, shouts and screams—then the silence.

She could almost feel the weight of the debris pushing

against her chest. Her entire body was tense. She wanted nothing more than to jump out and feel the sunlight on her cold body. She closed her eyes, and Dracon's face came instantly into focus. His soft, soothing words that night when he had rescued her had given her hope that she would survive.

Inhaling deeply, she forced her mind away from the wreckage. All she would think about was Dracon. He had saved her life. He had cared for her and never left her side. Which made why he had let her go so easily almost inconceivable. The breaths she had just managed to even out started coming again in short spurts. She opened her eyes as her father shifted in his seat. He was completely oblivious to her suffering. How could he be so indifferent to everything she'd endured?

By the time they arrived at Madeley Hall, she had exhausted herself with worry. But there was no time to contemplate a rest. No sooner had she alighted from the carriage than the front door swung open and her aunt came running out.

"Oh my," Aunt Rowena squealed with high-pitched excitement. "You are finally home. I was most anxious to return from Bath, all the while hoping you had received my letter and would return, and here you are."

Antonia stepped into her aunt's warm embrace. This was worth coming home for. She had missed Rowena more than she had ever realized. Too overwhelmed with emotion, she just enjoyed being held.

"Happy Christmas, Antonia." The sound of her ex-friend's voice sent a shiver down her spine. "We are so pleased that you are able to join us for our Yuletide celebrations."

Staying within her aunt's embrace, Antonia turned her

head toward the direction of the woman who had caused her so much grief. "Happy Christmas," she managed to mutter. The sight of her father wrapping his arm about Hester and guiding her back inside the house made her blood boil.

"Don't mind them, they often ignore everyone." Aunt Rowena hugged her again. "I am most pleased you have come home. But why did you stay away?"

There were some things she was not going to discuss with her aunt. She settled on a simplified version. "I was tired of Father dictating my every action. He even wanted me to give up playing the violin." Oh, the irony! Because she was in need of funds, she had been forced to sell the instrument. But Dracon had more than made up for that.

Why must her thoughts always stray back to him?

As they strolled toward the door, Aunt Rowena announced, "I am proud of you. It took courage to stand up to your father."

"Thank you, that means a lot to me." But something was still nagging her. "Why did you send the letter stating Father was ill?"

"Over the years, I asked your father to go after you, but my brother was being as stubborn as always. He was convinced you just needed time and that you would return home of your own volition. I knew you needed to be with your family, and that you needed an extra little push to come home."

Antonia offered a half smile. "I don't believe Father really cares for me."

Aunt Rowena stopped and faced her. "That is utter nonsense," she scolded. "Of course, he cares for you. But he is selfish. *His* wants and needs always come before everyone else's, as you well know."

"Except for Hester's." Antonia could hear the jealousy in her own voice, and it did not sit well with her.

Was she really jealous of Hester?

No. Jealousy was not at the root of the issue. She ached over the loss of her mother and all she had suffered at Father's hand.

All her life she had tried to be a good daughter, but nothing she did ever seemed good enough for her father. He had made every decision for her and thought nothing of dismissing her requests. Even her engagement to Dracon had been her father's idea. She had never had a say in anything that affected her life.

"You mustn't mind your father. He means well."

Aunt Rowena kept Antonia's arm firmly in the crook of her own as they ascended the grey stone steps. Flashbacks from her childhood flooded to the forefront of her mind. Her mother had made this house beautiful, but now the dark and dreary space held no such joy. Although Madeley Hall was richly appointed, it was devoid of all seasonal cheer. There was not one single evergreen to be seen.

"Are there to be no decorations?" She whispered her question with an uneasiness that she had not felt in a long time.

Her aunt leaned and whispered just as quietly, "The Yule log was brought in last night, but your father's wife does not care for any greenery. In fact, except for grand feasts, Lady Madeley does not enjoy most diversions."

It would appear that her father had indeed made a most splendid match.

⚜

CHAPTER 11

*D*racon knew letting Antonia return home with her father to celebrate Christmastide was the right decision, but in his heart, he wanted her here with him. Letting her go was the hardest thing he had ever done. There was a time and place to fight for what one wanted, and he knew she needed time with her father, to resolve the past. Besides, he needed time, too, to reflect upon Lord Madeley's anger toward him. The warning he had issued to Dracon only moments before Antonia appeared on the stairs was none too subtle. The blackguard actually threatened Dracon to stay away from his daughter, or else suffer at the tongues of gossips. Dracon would not lose Antonia because of more cruel rumors.

He went to the sideboard, grabbed a glass and a bottle of brandy, and retreated to his favorite chair.

How long should he wait before speaking to Lord Madeley about his intentions?

Antonia's world had been turned upside down, first by her mother's death, and then by the carriage accident. All Dracon wanted was what was best for her. Despite the intimacies they had shared, there was some unseen barrier between them he could not quite place.

Closing his eyes, he pinched the bridge of his nose, contemplating. Images of Antonia danced through his mind. He wanted nothing more than to have her here by his side. She filled the house with joy and music. Easing further into the chair, relaxing into its warm softness, he could almost hear her playing her violin.

My father never asked me what I wanted.

He bolted upright, his eyes opening wide at the revelation. He had already decided she would be his wife, but he had never asked her! He never asked what *she* wanted.

Jumping up from the chair, he left the empty glass and unopened bottle on the small table next to it and went to the Great Hall. Bess was still putting the finishing touches to the decorations for the fête for the staff when Dracon approached her.

"Do we have more greenery?"

"We have quite a bit still. What…?" A twinkle gleamed in Bess' eyes. "Might I assume what this is all about?"

There was no doubt or hesitation what Dracon's next course of action would be. "I want the white suite decorated… No, I will see to the white suite. You finish here." Dracon glanced about at him. What would make Antonia happy? "Is there still some white ribbon?"

"Yes, I believe there is." Bess rummaged through a pile of odds and ends for countless seconds before she exclaimed, "Here it is!"

Dracon took the offered ribbon while Bess smiled brightly. "It appears we might have a marchioness for Christmas," she said with a wink.

He returned her smile then gathered greenery, mistletoe,

and took the ribbon before going to the white suite. This was his task and his alone.

Hours later, he stood back and eyed his handiwork. There were still some final additions that he was not sure any man could achieve. He took a small box from his pocket and placed it on the mantel. He wanted everything to be in place and perfect when he brought Antonia home.

A firm knock sounded on the door before Bess entered. "I am surprised to still find you here."

He turned around to face the housekeeper. "What is that supposed to mean?"

She picked up a stray piece of evergreen from the floor. "I have watched the two of you growing closer over the past few days. I also saw the look of hurt and disappointment Antonia wore when she left with Lord Madeley this afternoon."

Dracon knew he had been wrong not to tell Antonia how he felt. After what they had shared, he had thought she would realize what his intentions were. Words of affection were never easy for him to express. Damn, he was a blundering idiot. In that moment, he had believed he was doing the right thing in sending Antonia home with her father. He was wrong.

"I know that you want to give her time with her family, but that doesn't mean you have to sulk here alone, my lord."

He was about to argue that he had not been sulking, when it dawned on him that he had—for the last five years. "Thank you, Bess. Inform Fulbert to have the carriage brought around."

"Yes, my lord," she said with a broad smile of approval.

Dracon wasted no time readying for the short journey. Thirty minutes later, he was ensconced in the carriage and on his way through the rain and sleet. It would have been faster

on horseback, but he fully intended on bringing Antonia back
to Lionshead with him tonight.

♪♪♪

ANTONIA REALIZED the seasonal festivities had been planned
well before her arrival, but the last thing she wanted to do
was to be social. She had hoped to have a quiet evening,
spending time with her father. But clearly, being alone with
his only daughter was the last thing on his mind. He was
more interested in impressing his prestigious guests.

Fortunately, she was able to find something to wear
amongst her old clothes. She did not care if she was out of
date; it was just ever so pleasant not to be wearing black. She
would not miss that façade.

As guests arrived, Antonia tried to be pleasant and cheery,
but it was clear that she was an intruder in her childhood
home. Only her aunt had made an effort to make her feel
welcome. With each passing minute, she hoped that Dracon
would storm through the door and whisk her away. But by the
time dinner was announced, it was clear he would not be
coming.

To make matters worse, she was paired with Lord Prendergast. During her first season, he had shown interest and
showered her with flowers, but then her mother's health
turned for the worse, and her season was cut short. Not that
she had any interest in the likes of Lord Prendergast. He was
far too stuffy and only concerned with himself. It was no
wonder her father liked the gentleman. They were cut from
the same cloth.

Out of the corner of her eye, she noticed Lord Prendergast
would not stop looking at her. Every time she glanced his

way, he offered a wide smile, revealing a mouth overly stuffed with crooked teeth. Her stomach lurched at his leering gaze.

"Lord Madeley informed me that you intend to stay at Madeley Hall permanently."

Antonia wanted to scream. Her father was doing it again. She knew it was commonplace for fathers to make decisions for their families, but she was never informed about anything, and seemed to always receive information about her life from someone other than her parent. She didn't know what the future held, but one thing was for certain, *she* was in charge of her destiny.

In as nonchalant a tone as she could muster, she said, "I haven't yet decided. Lady MacKinnon is expecting me to—"

"Who is Lady MacKinnon?" Lord Prendergast questioned as he served her a slice of roasted boar. The enticing aroma curdled Antonia's stomach under Prendergast's lascivious eye.

She no longer had any qualms about the past five years. She had told her father everything—well, not quite everything—although she had told him about her position as Lady MacKinnon's companion.

"My employer," she stated matter-of-factly. The look of horror on Prendergast's face prompted her to giggle.

"I do not see what is so amusing, Miss Madeley. A woman of your station should not be employed…" Prendergast went on a ten-minute rant, which Antonia somehow managed to turn a deaf ear to despite his loud tone. By the time he'd finished, her head was pounding. What was supposed to be a pleasant evening spent with family had turned into an ordeal, mostly surrounded by strangers.

By the time the Christmas pudding was served, she was ready to run from the room. And if that weren't bad enough, when the ladies departed while the men enjoyed cigars and brandy, Antonia found herself ignored. Even her aunt was engaged elsewhere.

Worn in body and spirit, she decided to sneak away, if only for a short while. Once the men rejoined them, Father was sure to notice her absence, and she would be forced to take part in the evening games.

She had barely left the drawing room when her father's firm voice called to her. "Antonia, might I have a word with you?"

So much for a moment's reprieve.

With some reluctance, she followed him to his study. She sat down on the large settee, wondering whatever could be so important that her father would neglect his duties as host to have a private moment alone with her.

"I have excellent news, daughter." His tone was full of arrogance and self-importance.

All the reasons why Antonia had run away came to mind once again. She sat perfectly still, with her hands folded in her lap, and waited.

He waved his hand with much fanfare and announced. "Lord Prendergast has offered for your hand this very evening."

"He what?" Her voice squeaked as anger pounded through her body.

"He has made a most generous offer, and I've accepted." The tone in her father's voice brooked no argument. "The banns will be posted and—"

The rising anger overtook her with such fury that she practically screamed at her father, hoping to be heard. "Father, I have only just returned and…" His eyes darkened as he sent her a silent warning. She softened her tone, knowing full well that he could destroy her future. "I was hoping to spend time with you before deciding on the future." That was the most she had ever spoken against her father in her entire life, and it felt wonderful.

"I've made up my mind. An offer like this won't come along again since you're practically on the shelf."

She lifted her chin, meeting his arrogant gaze. "What of Lord Trawden?"

The smug smile on her father's face sent a chill down her spine. "*He* has *not* offered for your hand." She'd never heard her father speak with such disdain and hatred. "You can not expect me to decline Lord Prendergast's offer with the hope that… that arrogant blackguard will come around."

"Don't call Dracon that," she screamed, all the frustration she had pent up over the years bursting through.

He strolled up to her, his manner calculatedly calm. "Even if he did ask for your hand, I would never approve of Lord Trawden."

"Did someone say my name?"

Antonia's heart stopped as Dracon entered the room, looking more handsome than she ever thought possible.

"You are just in time, Lord Trawden." Her father eyed Dracon nervously. "I was about to make an announcement to my guests." Father did not wait for either of them to respond, but strode past Dracon and headed toward the drawing room.

Antonia ran after him, desperate to stop him. "Father, please, can we not discuss this?" He didn't answer, but picked up his pace. She felt Dracon's presence close behind even before she heard his footsteps.

Grabbing at her father's sleeve, she pulled him to a halt. He spun on his heels, anger bright in his eyes. "My mind is made up," he growled. "You defied me once. Not again. I will not endure another season of rumors because of your behavior." His voice reverberated down the hall, drawing guests from the festivities. "You have always been a burden to me, just like your mother. Not again. You *will* do as I say," he growled.

The guests had spilled into the hall, struggling to see what the commotion was about.

"What's going on, Lord Madeley?" Dracon said in a deep, accusatory tone that halted all conversation and gaiety.

With a cynical calm her father announced, "I had hoped to make my announcement in a more comfortable environment, but since you insist, Lord Trawden, I shall make it here in the corridor."

Antonia put her hand on her father's sleeve. "Please, Father," she whispered. "Please don't do this."

He looked down at her, offered a slight grin, and then raised his head. "Friends, honored guests, it is my great joy to announce…"

Antonia's world tipped on its side as her father ignored her protests and prepared to humiliate her.

"… the engagement of my daughter to Lord Prendergast." Cheers and well-wishes rang through the hall.

"The hell you are." Everyone turned toward Dracon. "Miss Madeley belongs with me." Joy coursed through her veins—Dracon wanted to be with her!

"You had your chance, old chap," Prendergast said with a jovial smile that faded the moment Dracon turned a harsh gaze upon him.

"Antonia is mine." Dracon's possessive statement should have angered her, but instead it had the opposite effect, sending a jolt of excitement straight to her toes.

"I have already accepted Prendergast's offer," Lord Madeley interrupted, "and it stands. My daughter will marry—"

"Perhaps you misunderstood me." Dracon approached her father, towering over him. "I have already made her mine."

Gasps rang in unison. Did Dracon just announce to everyone that they had been intimate? Heat coursed through her body, warming her a dozen degrees. The room began to spin out of control. Closing her eyes, she brought her hand to her pounding temples. Voices swirled around her. Aunt Rowena wrapped a cloak about her and promised to visit once her brother's temper had cooled, and then Antonia was being whisked away to Dracon's waiting conveyance.

This was not how she had imagined her rescue.

CHAPTER 12

The ride back to Lionshead was torturous. Storm clouds had rolled in, consuming the landscape with their anger. It was too similar to the night of the accident. Worse still, Antonia was still fuming over Dracon's behavior. He had announced to everyone that he had ruined her, and then hurried her away from Madeley Hall.

Dracon had not said two words, but sat staring at her from one corner of the carriage. He looked as uncomfortable as she felt. She could not possibly imagine what he was thinking.

Say something. Anything!

Rain pummeled the conveyance, which swayed sharply to one side, causing Antonia to slide along the seat. Her thumping heart drowned out all other sounds, and everything around became hazy and out of focus.

Closing her eyes, she grabbed hold of the seat. "Please don't turn over, please. I don't want to die," she whispered into the night.

"Damn." She heard Dracon swear and in the next moment she was lifted up onto his lap.

She had no time to protest before he brought his mouth

down on hers in a hungry, soul-searching kiss. She could feel his arousal pressed against her bottom. She wanted to at least demand he apologize before she gave in to desire, but common sense had left her the moment his hand had cupped her breast. They'd only been apart half a day, but oh, did she miss him!

His velvety tongue explored and demanded she return all he gave. His hand slid down her side. When he reached the edge of her skirt, he began bunching it up until he had access to her heated skin. His hand roamed up her thigh and found the slit in her drawers. He slid one long finger inside, his thumb rubbing her sensitive spot.

"What are you doing?" She breathed against his lips in short gasps.

"Distracting you," he said with equally labored breaths.

"It's working." She wrapped her arms about his neck and pulled him into her. She shifted, desperate to get closer to him. All thoughts of the storm faded away and were replaced with a fiery ache and growing need to feel more of him.

Tugging at his cravat, she managed to undo it and toss it to one side. She began unbuttoning his vest and shirt, running her hand to feel his warm skin, and beating heart. She knew he wanted her, and at that moment, it was all that mattered.

He pulled at the edges of her bodice, ripping the fabric. "I'll buy you another," he said as he released her breasts. He moved his mouth over one, devouring its softness. Heat raced through her bloodstream; she had never felt anything so wonderful.

A needing ache pulsed where his hand had been. She pushed her body further into him, wanting to feel his heated skin against hers. There was a hunger in his eyes that thrilled her.

The carriage jerked, and she practically leapt off his lap.

The thrill of what they had been doing gave way to panic. Her chest felt as if it would break under the intense pounding of her heart. She couldn't seem to control the trembling that was consuming her.

He held her in place. "Shh, I won't let any harm come to you."

Without warning, she began to cry, and much to her dismay, not with delicate little sobs. Dracon gathered her into his arms and held her tight against him, kissing the top of her head and uttering soothing words until she settled.

Warmed by the heat of his embrace and comforted by his strong arms, she must have dozed, for the next thing she knew, the carriage had stopped in front of Lionshead, and Dracon was carrying her up the front steps. In the span of a week, she had entered this house twice, and both times Dracon had carried her. She buried her face into his chest, embarrassed by what the servants must think of her disheveled appearance.

He did not slow his pace, but took her straight to the room she had been occupying. He opened the door, carried her over the threshold, then kicked the door shut.

He set her down on the bed and then, much to her surprise, turned away from her. "I need to know *why* you left five years ago." She had begun to explain about her father when he added, "And don't tell me it had something to do with your father. I already know he is an irrepressible ass. What I want to know is *why* you left *me*?"

She was tired of hiding her feelings. Dracon cared for her, and that was enough. She could not expect more and was content just to be with him. Perhaps over time his feelings for her might deepen.

"Antonia? I want to know why." He ran a shaky hand through his dark hair. "Why did you leave?"

She brought her knees to her chin and wrapped her arms about her legs. She swallowed the hard lump in her throat. Damn, but she didn't think she could keep the truth from him any longer. Deep down, she didn't want to, but this was harder than she had thought it would be. She couldn't look at him and instead focused on the print of her dress. She took in a quick breath. "It is common knowledge how you felt about your late wife. I was scared."

"I didn't kill her," he ground out. "It was an accident." Raw pain contorted his features.

"I know that." She lifted her head and argued back. "It is not what this is about."

He paced back and forth several times before he ground out. "Then what the hell *is* this all about?"

She gritted her teeth and cried, "I can't compete with her!"

He stilled. "What are you talking about?" His piercing blue eyes held such pain and grief. Grief for the woman he lost…

"Catherine. I know how much you loved her, and it scared me." Antonia practically shouted the words. "I know you could never love me the way you loved her, but—"

"Damn it, Antonia. I never loved her the way I love you."

"Wh…wh…" Antonia stuttered before she managed, "What did you say?"

Dracon came up and sat on the edge of the bed. Wiping away her tears, he repeated, "I love you, my Antonia. I love you like none other."

Her mind was still trying to comprehend what he'd just revealed. "I don't understand. Everyone said that you and…"

Dracon took in an unsteady breath. "Catherine and I cared for one other, but we were never in love. Ours was a marriage of convenience. She wanted to have children, and, at the time,

I wanted an heir. That duty had been instilled in me for as long as I could remember."

"I don't understand. Miss…" She cleared her throat. "Everyone had always spoken about your love match." Her mind was trying to put all the pieces together. "It wasn't true?"

"Catherine was a friend. We grew up together. Our families expected us to marry, and I didn't think any differently. I would never have done anything to harm her. That night she…" His words broke off and he turned away.

She reached for him and rubbed his arm. "You don't have to talk about it." His muscles tensed under her hand.

"I *need* to tell you." He looked into her eyes with intensity. "I *want* to tell you."

She leaned in and kissed his cheek.

"She was so excited about feeling the baby move, she came running down the stairs." His voice was shaking. "She stumbled and fell. I thought my world ended that night." He took Antonia's hands in his. "Until I saw you. I had been dead inside for so long and you brought me back to life."

"How did I—"

"When I heard you play your violin."

"You like my music?" The thought thrilled her. Whenever she played the violin, she felt alive. And Dracon felt the same?

"You play with such passion. I was mesmerized. I wanted to court you, but your father insisted on a hasty engagement."

She let out a laugh. "I was furious with him. I was still mourning the loss of my mother and then he announced his engagement to Miss Uppington, and then… it was all happening too fast. My stepmother, and then Miss Rede said—"

"My late wife's cousin? What did she say?" His expression was clouded with anger.

Antonia hesitated. She did not want to bring up the past, but… "Miss Rede is the one who convinced me to run away."

Dracon looked as if he were about to explode with anger.

"She said that you were deeply in love with your late wife, and you were only interested in marrying because you desired an heir. That's why my father married my mother. I didn't want to end up like her."

Dracon cupped her cheek, the warmth from his hand sending a tingle down her body. "I will never treat you as your father treated your mother." He kissed her forehead. "I promise to do everything within my power to make you happy." He kissed her cheek. "I love you, *my Antonia*." His last words were branded on her lips, his vow sealed with a soft, sensual kiss.

She ran her hand up his firm, sinewy arm, relishing in his strength. She settled her fingers behind his neck, encouraging him closer to her, but instead of reciprocating, he pulled away.

Resting his forehead to hers, he inhaled deeply. "Wait here."

He eased off the bed and strolled to the white mantel decorated with garlands of ivy interlaced with white and silver ribbons. Tears stung the corner of her eyes. *He remembered*. He retrieved a small box and returned to her side.

"I bought this for you—"

"You don't need to give me anything," Antonia interrupted. He'd already given her so much, she did not need gifts.

He silenced her protests with a gentle kiss. "Five years ago, I bought this as a symbol of my affection for you." He opened the box.

Staring back at her was the most beautiful brooch she had ever seen. The violin was perfectly detailed down to the strings, and across the upper bout was a delicately placed diamond-encrusted bow.

She met his loving eyes. Five years ago, she had convinced herself that Dracon could not ever care for her the way he had his first wife, but nothing could have been further from the truth. He took the brooch from the silk-lined box and pinned it on her.

"It was supposed to be a wedding gift, but perhaps it could be an engagement present." He took her hands in his. "Marry me, my Antonia."

Tears streamed down her cheeks. Never in her wildest dreams would she ever have imagined being this happy. "Yes." She flung her arms about his neck and kissed him. "I love you, *my* Dracon."

EPILOGUE

New Year's Day

The day had not begun auspiciously, but by the time they were ready to leave for the church, the dark grey clouds had given way to a brilliant blue sky. A light layer of snow blanketed the landscape, sparkling like a thousand diamonds against the sunlight.

Not for the first time, Antonia wondered if she were living a fantasy. She was about to be married to the man who had made all her dreams come true, who shared her love for music, who had saved her from her own foolish mistakes.

The carriage came to a gentle halt in front of the small, ivy-covered church. Antonia descended after her father. Despite his initial protest, her father had eventually given his blessing. Their relationship would never be close, but at least the past had been laid to rest.

The moment she entered the church, all eyes turned toward her, but she only had eyes for Dracon. He was the most handsome, gentle, caring man in the world, and he loved her. As she walked down the aisle, the heat of his stare sent a ripple of excitement through her. He looked as if he was undressing her with his delicious blue eyes. She used to think they reminded her of the surface of water, but there was so much more depth in them, deeper than an ocean.

When she approached the altar he whispered, "You look beautiful."

His comment earned a disapproving glare from the curate who, after clearing his throat with much ceremony, began, "Dearly beloved, we are gathered here…"

His words faded as Antonia's mind drifted. Never before had she been this blissfully happy or felt this fully alive. It had truly been a long lesson to learn, and she was thankful each and every day that she had been given another chance at love with Dracon. He was all things to her.

They spoke their vows with deep reverence, and when the time came for Dracon to place the ring on her finger, the utter joy she had been trying to contain consumed her and bubbled over. She could not keep the smile from her face or the tears from her eyes.

He slid the gold ring engraved with music notes on the fourth finger of her left hand and held it there.

"With this Ring I thee wed, with my Body I thee worship, and with all my worldly Goods I thee endow. I love you with my body, my soul, and my heart, *my Antonia*."

And though it was not tradition, Dracon sealed his vow with a kiss.

* * *

I hope you enjoyed
A Marchioness for Christmas!

Keep reading for a sample of
When the Marquess Returns

A Legend to Love: Book 1

Chapter One

London, May 1819

The moment Maximus, his brother, and their adoptive mother entered the spacious hall of the grand theatre, curious eyes settled on them and murmurs encircled their small party.

Stares were commonplace whenever they entered a room, especially in this new environment. It had always been the case, although the novelty usually wore off within a couple of minutes. However, there was one lady in particular who kept her gaze centered on them, puzzlement streaked across her face. She tilted her brow, looking at them with uncertainty, almost as if she were trying to understand something. She didn't attempt to approach but continued to peer intently at them.

"Why is that woman staring at us?" Maximus questioned under his breath, barely able to keep the annoyance at bay.

"Perhaps she's never seen twins before," Lucius rebuffed.

Maximus and Lucius were not just twins, they were identical and—according to the local girls in the small village close to their childhood home near Plymouth—were "two of the most handsome men alive, and completely swoon-worthy". It was a moniker that Maximus did not care for, never had and probably never would. He'd rather be known for his intelligence, or skill with a horse, or knowledge of multiple languages, not for something as fleeting as appearance.

"Perhaps you remind her of someone. Just ignore," Larentia, their mother, said with nonchalance and a slight wave of her hand. "These women of the *ton* are often far too absorbed in gossip. Besides, we've only just arrived in Town. It couldn't possibly have anything to do with us."

"Miss St. Albans!" a cheerful voice crescendoed above the crowd bringing even further attention to their party. A rather plump woman dressed in deep purple scurried towards them. "You've finally returned to London."

"Lady Kenton," Larentia took the woman's hands in her own. "It has been too long, my dearest friend."

"Twenty-three years too long to be exact." The woman's warm smile settled on Maximus and his brother. "These must be your adopted sons. It is a pleasure to meet you both at long last. Larentia has written to me often of your adventures. Tell me, how did you enjoy your time on the Continent?"

Their time touring Europe felt like a lifetime ago. When their adoptive grandfather announced he wanted Maximus and Lucius to follow in his footsteps and embark on the Grand Tour, the brothers were just nineteen and—in Maximus's opinion—naïve about the world beyond Plymouth. It had been a time of great personal growth for each of them. He'd enjoyed visiting new places, experiencing local customs, honing his drafting skills, and spending time with his brother, but he'd always longed for more. However, before he could conclude what 'more' encompassed, they'd been summoned home.

So much had happened since they'd returned two years ago.

"It was most enjoyable," Maximus answered in a tone he hoped did not invite further questions. He was not in the mood for reminiscing, for sharing those intimate details of their travels, with someone he'd just met.

His brother on the other hand…

"I particularly enjoyed the opera in Milan, *e le belle*

donne," Lucius said before adding his infamously charming smile that quite frequently landed him in trouble.

"*Ricorda il nostro accordo*," Maximus warned under a hushed tone as Lady Kenton watched their exchange with interest. The brothers had already argued once today about Lucius's indiscretions since arriving in London a few days previous.

Lucius raised a brow in defiance, but kept his tone jovial. "*Lei non capisce l'italiano*."

"Oh my, and you both speak Italian?" A slight giggle escaped Lady Kenton's mouth as a deep blush stained her entire face. Turning back to Larentia, she said, "I have not a clue what they are saying, however, I do believe the mamas had best keep a close watch on their daughters with your sons in Town this season."

Larentia shot Maximus and Lucius her best "behave yourself" warning before clearing her throat. "The play is about to begin."

"Oh yes, and it should be quite a spectacular performance this evening. Madame Hébert is performing the aria this evening." The trio followed Lady Kenton up the grand staircase toward her box, passing even more curious eyes. "We'll have plenty of time to get acquainted later."

The gentle hum of conversation and general merriment that had filled the theatre lessened—only slightly—as the production began. Even as Maximus tried to focus on the stage and ignore the chatter echoing across the vast gold and green space, his mind wandered, contemplating the disagreement he'd had with his brother earlier regarding Lucius's current paramour. The woman in question had actually snuck into their townhome and cornered Maximus, believing *he* was Lucius. Then, upon discovering they were identical twins, offered her services to both brothers.

Maximus lost his temper with the woman, which angered his brother.

Why did he and his twin have to constantly be at odds? It never had been this way until their grandfather had passed away and they'd learned they would have to leave St. Albans Manor for London. Looking back, something had begun to change with Lucius that day.

Maximus adjusted himself for the umpteenth time, swiveling this way and that, trying to find a comfortable position. It wasn't that the seat was uncomfortable, or that he could even place blame on his surroundings—despite all the stares, it was that *he* was uncomfortable; uncomfortable and restless.

He stretched his legs and, in the process, made contact with his brother's chair. Two glaring blue eyes met his. "What is wrong with you?" Lucius's scold rumbled above the performance.

He shook his head, brushing off his brother's question. They'd already had one argument this evening, and he would be damned if they had another—and this one not in the privacy of their home. He couldn't do that to Larentia…again.

Damn. Why couldn't he relax?

He turned his focus to the stage, trying to enjoy… Hell, he couldn't even recall what he was supposed to be enjoying. A long sigh escaped his lips, earning a glare from all in their box. He attempted to adjust his legs again, this time kicking his brother's ankle. Lucius eyed him with annoyance, his mouth opened as if to argue, then he snapped it shut.

This was pointless.

Maximus left the box before he annoyed his brother further, and ducked into the hall, his muscles instantly relaxing. Perhaps he just wasn't used to the city. Except for those couple of years spent traveling across the Continent, he had spent little time in any city, much preferring quiet country life. A quick walk should ease whatever was plaguing him.

Strolling casually, ignoring the couple of theatregoers loitering at the far end of the hall, he began to make his way toward the grand staircase. Before he reached his destination, a muffled argument from one of the boxes halted his retreat.

No sooner had the sounds reached his ear when a woman stormed out of the box in question, colliding with him. He wrapped his arm about her waist to keep her from landing on the floor. They stood chest to chest, hearts beating rapidly.

"Oh," she gasped. "I…" Her words halted as she glanced up at him. Warm vanilla and sweet lavender encircled them.

Maximus stared into the most enticing eyes he'd ever seen—one emerald green, one deep brown. Her compelling eyes riveted him in place as his heart pounded against his chest anew.

Time halted, and energy surged between them. She stared at him with a tender longing.

Who was this woman?

Countless moments later, the lady spoke. "I apologize for ruining—"

"You didn't ruin anything," he quickly reassured her, but couldn't the find words to say more.

Her mouth curved into a beautiful smile, revealing matching dimples, which sent a whirlwind through his world. He'd always had a fondness for dimples. "I…I best be returning to my party."

"I suppose I should release you," he said with reluctance.

"Yes, I suppose," the words brushed past her pink lips with the same reluctance.

Several seconds passed before he actually did release her, his body instantly feeling the loss. Before he could ask her name, she retreated back into the box, leaving him wondering what the hell had just happened. If not for the remnants of lavender and vanilla clinging to his coat, he might have believed he dreamt the entire scene.

He paced a short length several times trying to convince himself he should *not* sneak into the box and discover her identity. *They had not been properly introduced. It would create a scene.* In the end, common sense won, and he decided it was best to rejoin his party.

Maximus took in a deep breath, the muscles tightening in chest, as he reluctantly walked back to his box.

"So nice of you to join us again." His brother's tone was laced with sarcasm as Maximus entered the loge. "I hope you've settled down."

His patience was being tested at every turn this evening. Before he could remark, Larentia stated, "Lady Kenton has offered to show us around Town later this week. Perhaps we may see the Egyptian Hall."

Maximus simply nodded as he took his seat. He had other things on his mind presently. He desperately wanted to discover more about the woman he'd encountered in the hall, and what had caused her to be so upset, and….

His heart sank. What if she was married and had quarreled with her husband? If that were the case, it was probably fortunate he hadn't barged in on her party. Before too long, he had conjured an entire scenario that had him enraged and wanting to call out the bastard who had upset her.

Damn. He needed to stay calm. He didn't even know her name. What if she wasn't married? How would he discover her identity without a proper introduction? He pondered the question for several minutes before an idea struck.

As soon as the play finished, he would rush to her box and casually bump into her again. It was a simple plan without the possibility of scandal. He would be able to talk to her again, and with any luck, acquire her name.

With his plan settled, he rather impatiently waited for the play to end. At least this time he knew what was disrupting his senses—a blonde-haired beauty, with the most intriguing eyes, four boxes away.

Loud clapping thundered through the theatre bringing him back to the present. Larentia and Lady Kenton were deep in conversation about the quality of the play and Madame Hébert's performance, while Lucius seemed distracted by something, or rather someone, near the stage.

Adrenaline rushed through his veins. There was no time to lose. He would worry about the next step once he found her again.

Emerging into the hall, excitement quickly gave way to frustration as his progress was hindered by several parties loitering in the hall engaging in lively talk about the evening's festivities, both on stage and in the audience. Maximus edged around them and waited near the box the lady had retreated to. With each passing minute, he became more anxious as more and more people filled the corridor. He watched as Larentia and Lady Kenton strolled past, and Lucius disappeared in the opposite direction. He could not be bothered with his brother's antics at the moment. Besides, he was his twin, not his keeper. He watched as the crowd dispersed and still no one emerged from box number four.

His insides turned as he struggled to formulate a new plan. Perhaps he could enter the loge, mistaking it for his own, claiming he'd forgotten…well, he didn't know what, he'd conjure some item when the time came. He maneuvered past the strolling guests, sucked in his breath, and pulled back the curtain.

Empty.

A heavy sigh escaped his lips. Where had she gone?

* * *

"Renovations on the cottage are almost complete. You'll finally be able to leave Warrington Hall."

"I enjoy spending time with Lady March," Sabina corrected her brother. Plus, she couldn't imagine being alone day after day, removed from Warrington Hall and those she held dear.

Titus ignored her comment, continuing on to extol the positives of the renovation. "I believe you will be most pleased with the small library," he said with much enthusiasm.

Since her lifelong dream to marry and have a family of her own would never be, it was nice to know that she would have a lovely cottage, far away from the gossips, to call her own. Despite her circumstances, she still fared better than most spinsters, thanks to her brother. He might be several years younger than her, but once he reached his majority, he had always ensured her future was secure.

Before she could express her appreciation for what Titus had arranged, her sister-in-law—Eunice, interfered. "The final steps into spinsterhood," she said with a snicker. "And a fitting end for the Cursed Heiress."

"Eunice, that's enough," Titus half-scolded. Sabina could not blame her brother for not taking a firmer approach with his wife. He had to endure her—and their mother—every day he took a breath, not to mention still being in need of an heir. She truly felt for him.

"You shouldn't take that tone with your wife," their mother said as she took Eunice's hand, lovingly folding it within her own.

Eunice raised a triumphant chin before taking another jab at Sabina's expense. "I suppose living the life of a spinster in the old hunting cottage *is* better than being at Lady March's side constantly." Eunice clearly had learned the disagreeable art of insulting Sabina from her husband's mother. For two women not related, the similarities and jibes were endless.

As if enduring her sister-in-law wasn't trying enough, Mother decided it was her turn to chime in, "I still can't quite comprehend how you managed to swindle His Grace and Lady March into letting you reside with them all these years."

Mustering what little bravado she had left in her soul, Sabina retorted, "Perhaps if you had been more—"

Mother's eyes turned ice cold and filled with hatred. "What? More of a mother?" She clutched her hand to her chest, her performance rivaling those of the actors on stage. "I was grieving the loss of my husband."

"And my father." Sabina shook her head, trying to erase the memory of that horrible day and her mother's unkind words. She did not want to suffer another lecture, followed by an argument, and conclude with more insults. Instead she settled for a plea. "I rarely see you and Titus. Do you not think it possible that we could have a pleasant evening just this once, Mother?"

"I agree with Sabina." For the second time that evening, her brother came to her defense, but she was certain he would pay the price later.

"Of course you do," cried Eunice. "You always side with your *dearest* sister. You don't care for me." Sniffling, she buried her face in her hands.

Or sooner it would seem.

"There, there, Eunice, darling." Sabina's mother, the woman who'd given birth to her, who was supposed to love her, was comforting the instigator. Mother raised her gaze to

Sabina. "Look what you've done." Hatred blazed in her eyes. "What have *I* done to deserve a daughter like you? I've been cursed since the day you were born."

The words seared straight through Sabina's heart, striking at her very core. Tears burned the corners of her eyes as she fought to control her breathing. One would think she would be used to the barbs after enduring so many years of them, but they still hurt. Since her father's passing, all she had ever wanted was her mother's love.

Desperate to escape, even if only for a moment to regain her composure, Sabina swallowed the hard lump in her throat, raised her chin, pulled back the curtain, rushed from their box none-too-gracefully, and straight into a wall. Only this wall was warm and smelled like a pleasant autumn afternoon in the country.

Firm arms wrapped about her waist, keeping her from falling. She glanced up into the most handsome face she'd ever seen.

"Oh…I…I'm…" She sounded like such a ninny instead of a woman of thirty.

She lost herself in the sea of his clear blue eyes. The theatre, her mother's cruel words, the constant stares, all faded away and settled into this one perfect moment. His warm hands penetrated through her satin dress, searing her skin and sent her heart thundering.

She tried to think of something intelligent—or at least somewhat witty—to say but she was not used to conversing with handsome men who disrupted her senses. "I…I apolo-gize for ruining—"

"You didn't ruin anything," the handsome stranger's deep masculine voice quickly set her at ease. His fervent gaze stirred a long-forgotten flutter in her stomach.

She did not want the moment to end but did not want him

to be caught with her either. She fought to control her swirling emotions. "I best be returning to my party."

"I suppose I should release you." It almost sounded like he didn't want to.

Her heart soared for a brief moment before reality pierced it with an arrow, sending it crashing to the ground. Although there was something familiar about him that she couldn't quite place, it was clear this gentleman was new to London, otherwise he would have already set her to her feet, bid adieu, and run the other way. The gossipmongers could be altogether too cruel to those who came near the Cursed Heiress.

"Yes, I suppose," she whispered. Despite the glorious feel of his warm hands holding her, it *was* for the best. Her life's path was clear, straight and narrow.

Although not quite ready to face her family, she slipped quietly into the box and took her seat, praying her mother might have some compassion for her frayed nerves.

"So, you've decided to return?" Mother's tone was hard and disapproving.

Sabina had hoped to have a pleasant visit with her brother, but current company made it impossible. Rigidly holding her tears in check, she tried to maintain her composure for peering eyes, tried to ignore her mother's slights and Eunice's harsh glare, tried to ignore the stares and hushed mockery from the gossipmongers, but she was only human.

Mustering whatever calmness still within her power, she politely excused herself. It was the one positive aspect to being a spinster—she could come and go as she pleased. No sooner had she retreated down the grand staircase than curious onlookers were weaving tales about the Cursed Heiress. She picked up her pace and never looked back.

ABOUT THE AUTHOR

Award winning historical romance author Alanna Lucas grew up in Southern California, but always dreamed of distant lands and bygone eras. From an early age, she took an interest in history and travel, and is thrilled to incorporate those diversions into her writing. Alanna writes Regency-set historical romance.

When she is not daydreaming of her next travel destination Alanna can be found researching, spending time with family, or going for long walks. She makes her home in California with her husband, children, one sweet dog, and hundreds of books.

Just for the record, you can never have too many shoes, handbags, or books. And travel is a must.

Find Alanna online at www.alannalucas.com

🄵

ALSO BY ALANNA LUCAS

When the Marquess Returns

A Legend to Love: Book 1

A Marquess in Waiting and the Cursed Heiress…

The *ton* is abuzz and mamas are lining up their daughters; identical twins Maximus and Lucius St. Albans are making their entry into society. But they're not just eligible—they're the missing grandsons of the Duke of Warrington, stolen as infants.

However, Maximus doesn't relish the battle with his cocky, reprobate brother to be the next Marquess. And he has no time for the simpering misses now vying for his attention. Only Miss Sabina Teverton has his interest.

She was resigned to life as a spinster but from the moment Sabina meets Lord Maximus, her heart is torn. She dreams of a match with him—but how can that be when she's been branded as cursed…and she knows secrets of that night long ago when Maximus and his twin were snatched from their cradles?

* * *

Tempting Lord Lucias

A Legend to Love Novella: Book 2

Once, Lord Lucius St. Albans was a notorious rake. But since a horse racing accident that nearly killed him, mistresses and gambling hells have lost their allure. His long-lost grandfather, the

Duke of Warrington, has given him Ashby Manor, which Lucius longs to fill with a loving wife and children. His redemption is almost complete.

Although she barely casts him a second glance, he finds Miss Adele Sutherland utterly bewitching. But as far as Adele is concerned, Lord Lucius is to be swerved; her younger sister was ruined by a seducer of a similar ilk. She will keep to her quiet life of raising her young nephew and running the family stables. However, when Lucius requests riding tuition, she just cannot afford to turn away his business, so she vows to use every ounce of strength she possesses *not* to be tempted by his legendary charm.

Only Adele hasn't bargained on discovering that Lucius is a far kinder, sweeter man than his rakish reputation…Or that he's the one person who may come to her assistance when all that she cherishes is threatened with going up in smoke…

Manufactured by Amazon.com.au
Sydney, New South Wales, Australia